MEDUSA'S SON SERIES BOOK 2

THE MEDUSA DIVISION

IAN MITCHELL-GILL

This is a work of fiction. Names, characters, places, and incidents are products of the author's imagination or are used fictitiously and are not to be construed as real. Any resemblance to actual events, locations, organizations, or persons, living or dead, is entirely coincidental.

World Castle Publishing, LLC
Pensacola, Florida
Copyright © 2024 Ian Mitchell-Gill
Paperback ISBN: 9798891262508
eBook ISBN: 9798891262515
First Edition World Castle Publishing, LLC, August 12, 2024
http://www.worldcastlepublishing.com

Licensing Notes

Cover: Cover Designs by Karen
Cover-designs-by-karen.com
Editor: Karen Fuller

CHAPTER 1

Moscow in winter is a sight. A mix of pure snow falling in the street lights, moving vehicles, and Russians living as only Russians know how.

A good hat, warm coat, and a warmer companion on my arm made for a nice walk on the streets. Our boots crunched the packed snow on the sidewalk. I felt Irina's arm holding mine and her head leaning on my shoulder. Her long, dark hair collected snowflakes while her earmuffs kept her ears warm.

She was sleeping better and coping with memories nobody should own. She'd been through more than most and had come out the other side intact but a changed woman. She looked eighteen, but she had twenty lost years that nobody could get back. She'd been a monster, a vampire, and you can't just pretend it never happened. It would haunt anybody.

I'd changed, too. Killing people, being drained of blood daily, running with the Yakuza in Japan … it all leaves a mark. I was death on two legs for the vampire nation. But I never wanted that role, and I never wanted anyone to die because of me. As good as I'd been for Irina, I needed her too. Who else could understand?

We almost fell when a large figure in a black coat and red scarf stumbled in the snow and bumped into us. She held on to me, and I gently straightened my arms, easing the figure back into balance. I looked at his face. A brutish nose with broken blood vessels and mean little eyes. He scowled at me and growled, "*Smotret' kuda ty idesh'*!"

"Very sorry, friend. *Izvinyayus.*" I said with a smile. I looked at Irina. Her dark eyes were wide, and she was breathing a little faster. *Uh oh*!

"*Amerikanskiy*?" he snarled, and spat on the sidewalk. I figured saying nothing was the best course of action or inaction.

He turned his head and glowered at Irina, who glared right back. He sneered at her, "*Chto ty smotrish' na suku!*" he barked.

I winced and closed my eyes. Ugh, big mistake. Why did he have to say *that* to *her*? I looked at Irina, but she wasn't at my side. Her mitts were off and she had the big lout by the collar and quickly threw him clear across the busy street. He sailed over the cars driving on the road, arms and legs flailing, and landed in a pile of snow and garbage.

Irina took a step towards him, and I moved forward to put my gloved hands on her shoulders. She chose to stop. We both knew I couldn't hold her if she decided to get to him.

"Hey, little dove," I said, using her father's pet name for her. "He deserved that. He did … but nothing more. Okay?"

All the hostility ran away from her face. Those rich, black eyes softened, and a small smile touched the corners of her mouth. "Okay, Walt," she said with that sultry Russian accent.

"Your father is waiting at the restaurant for us, remember?" I offered her my arm, and she took it again.

She leaned her head on my shoulder once more as we resumed walking. "I am hungry, and it will be good to see Papa."

"It's always good to see your father. I hear the restaurant is quite nice. It's run by your uncle?"

"Da, uncle Yuri runs restaurant."

We walked in silence for a couple of minutes. She tugged on my arm and looked up at me. "That was good throw, yes?"

"Yes, it really was. Nice shot, hitting that pile of garbage and the snow."

She didn't look at me as we kept walking. "I did not see garbage or snow," she confessed.

"Oh, well ... it was still a good throw."

CHAPTER 2

Café Pushkin was *the* restaurant in Moscow. Everybody knew that, and everybody wanted a table, but reservations were not easy to get. You had to know somebody.

We saw the nineteenth-century baroque mansion, looked at each other, and smiled. There was a line, and we joined it, waiting for our chance to talk to the Maître De. I could feel a few eyes on us, wondering what two young people were doing at such an esteemed establishment. I was about to turn nineteen, and Irina was a young-looking eighteen.

Our turn came, and we stepped up. The man was wearing an elegant black tuxedo, and he was tall and thin. His hair was short and streaked with grey. He raised an eyebrow and said, *"Dobryy vecher. Nazovite pozhaluysta?"*

"Kamenev. Menya zovut Irina Kamenev," she answered with a strong voice. There was pride in her delivery, and she looked the man right in the eyes. It

was so easy to love her.

The man's eyes widened, and he blinked at us a couple of times. A fake, reptilian smile spread across his face, but I saw a little fear. "*Vash stol zhdet.*"

He turned and gestured for us to follow. He took us to a place called the Library Hall. I looked around, and I liked what I saw. Green tablecloths on every table, and the wooden chairs had matching cushions. The carpet looked ancient and intricate, but the most appealing thing was the bookshelves. Chestnut brown bookshelves were installed into the four pillars in the middle of the cozy restaurant and stretched right up to the roof. Antique lamps on the table, the ornate crown molding on the old tin roof … it was incredible. What a restaurant!

The Maître De took us to a table for four, and Irina's father was waiting for us. He was wearing his blue suit with the red star pin on the lapel. His hair was slicked back, and he was reading a menu. Was this business or pleasure? He looked up as we got close, and he stood, smiling ear to ear. "Ah, hello to you both," he said and walked toward us, arms wide.

The big Russian embraced his delicate daughter and kissed her on the forehead. I couldn't hear what he said to her. It was quiet, tender, and just for her. Then he turned to me and gave me a bear hug. The power in that old body was surprising. "So good to see you,

Walt."

"You too, Comrade," I grunted.

He held me at arm's length. "When will you call me Ivan?"

"Someday," I laughed. "This restaurant is amazing."

Kamenev shrugged and gestured for us to sit. "It is good to have family who can get us a table at such a place. Irina's uncle, Yuri, is important here."

I looked around as we sat and saw people checking out the big man's guests. "Really? Why do I feel like you are important, too? You never did tell me your official role in the government."

There was a gleam in his eye as he smiled at me from across the table. "No, you never did ask my official role." He lifted the menu and pointed at it. "There are some lovely appetizers you should consider."

Irina and I laughed. It was clear that he was not going to divulge any information of any kind. I'd probably never know, and it didn't really matter anyway. He ranked high. That was clear in the way everyone talked to him.

We took our menus, but Kamenev turned to his daughter. "Are you sleeping well, little dove? You look rested."

I held up a hand. "It's okay if you want to speak in Russian. I don't mind."

Irina frowned and shook her head, and her father did the same. It was almost comical how similar their facial expression and movement was. Even if they didn't have the same dark eyes, it was obvious he was her father.

"Nyet, that would be rude," our host explained.

I laughed and shook my head, too. "No. You two have waited twenty years to sit at such a beautiful restaurant together. Nothing is more special than a father's love for his daughter." I looked at them both and smiled. "Talk to each other in your mother tongue. It will give me time to read the menu."

Irina reached out and took his hand, and they both looked at me. The big Russian smiled and nodded. "Thank you, Walt."

It was nice to hear them talking to each other as I looked over the food choices. Irina talked so much faster when she was speaking her own language and their tone was gentle. A waiter wearing a dress shirt, green vest, and apron came and interrupted, but nobody minded. Irina ordered first, helped me understand some of the words on the menu that I didn't know, and our host ordered last. He added something as the waiter was about to leave.

A moment later, the waiter came with a bottle of red wine and three glasses. He pulled the cork and allowed Irina's father to smell it. Kamenev approved, and the waiter poured the wine and left.

"Try it. It is a very nice vintage," our host explained.

We all had a sip, and our eyes lit up. It was delicious. "*Spacibo, Comrade*! It is a wonderful wine. We almost don't need anything else."

"Nyet, dinner is required. We must eat as we talk. I have something important to discuss with you."

Irina and I gave each other a quick glance. "Is everything okay?" I asked.

Kamenev smiled and held up his glass. "*Da*! I want to offer you a job."

CHAPTER 3

I looked around the restaurant at the antique books on the shelves and back at our host. "Why is it I don't think the job you are offering has to do with a library or books?"

Kamenev laughed. "That would suit you, no doubt. But you are right, I am offering you both a different kind of work. It is not for the faint of heart."

Conversation stopped as the waiter delivered our appetizers. We thanked him, and he bowed before turning and moving to another table. I took a bite of the appetizer Irina had picked for me and smiled at her. "Delicious. *Spacibo!*" Casting an eye at Kamenev, I gave him a half smile. "Okay, what would you like me to do?"

The Russian took a belt of the rich red wine and looked at both of us. "This is a job that would require both of you. You would be working together. I know better than to try and separate you."

Irina looked at me with those enormous eyes,

and I'm sure mine were a little bigger. Where was he going with this? "Again, what would we be doing?"

Our host cast his eyes at the next table, and the four men eating set down their cutlery dabbed their faces with their napkins, and hastily stood and left the restaurant. Did he just dismiss a table to keep our discussion private?

The big old warrior leaned forward and put his elbows on the table. "The vampires are broken. They no longer have the influence they once had in the big cities. Many of the younger creatures have turned themselves in, and we continue to try and help them. Some are cured, and some die, but that is the accord we have struck."

He picked up his wine and glowered at it as he swirled the red liquid in the crystal glass. "Some of the older monsters have gone into hiding. Some choose to lay low in the largest cities, while others have taken over small towns and villages in remote areas of the world."

I leaned forward, too. "And you want us to deal with them?"

He gave me a tight-lipped smile. "Da, I think you two would be perfect to lead a team to deal with such things."

Irina and I looked at each other, and I couldn't help but laugh. "Okay, I thought you would want me to take some action regarding vampires, but to lead? You must be joking."

He shook his head. "I can think of no one better."

"Who do you think would follow a nineteen-year-old American with no training ... in anything?"

Kamenev leaned back in his chair and grinned at me. "You underestimate yourself. There are many who would confidently follow 'Medusa's Son' into a confrontation with vampires."

"Okay, I understand why that would be an advantage, and people might get behind that. But why should I lead? Because of my blood? Because of my DNA?"

He arched an eyebrow at me. "You saved Harada. You helped find a treatment for those recently infected and saved my daughter, who had been suffering for twenty years. But more than that, you somehow did it under the very nose of the Yakuza. You are shrewd enough to deal with these devils. That much is clear."

I bit my lip and thought about that. A sip of my own wine was needed to gather my thoughts. It really was great. "I understand why you would want me involved. Why Irina? You really want your own daughter dealing with vampires? Hasn't she suffered enough?"

He looked at the beauty beside me. "She is stronger than any of them. You have seen it with your own eyes. Her enhanced senses make her a formidable huntress, and she has the motivation necessary when it comes to killing the things. If the time comes, she will not hesitate."

"You want us to kill them all?"

"No ... only when necessary. I want you to assess a problem, look for solutions, get those who are infected to submit to treatment." His face grew dark. "The old fiends must be destroyed as they will never surrender."

I rubbed my chin as I thought about his offer. "Why would I do this? I have a nice, peaceful life now. I read, write, and help Irina understand a world that is twenty years older than the one she remembers. What makes you think I would accept?"

Kamenev looked at Irina and said something quickly in Russian. Her eyes protested, but she rose and looked at me. "I have been asked to go to the restroom. You will excuse me, yes?"

I looked back at her father with narrowed eyes. "Sure, Irina. I get it."

We both watched her leave. The second she was out of earshot, her father turned to me and spoke. "Walt, I am so grateful for everything you have done for her. She is sleeping, and her time with you has helped her adjust. She needs something that you cannot give her."

"What?"

"An outlet for that rage. I know you feel it, too. It lurks just below her skin, and it eats at her soul. You know how much she hates these things. Let her release that fury in a way that benefits the world ... and her."

I sighed, "Comrade, you know killing is not in my nature. How can you think I want to be a part of such a thing?"

He laughed and tapped a finger on the table. "That is exactly right. I believe that these creatures will listen to a living legend and submit to the treatment. They know what you are. Survival is always their goal, and they will see your offer as being in their best interest."

"And Irina destroys any of them who refuse or any of the old guard?"

Kamenev spread his hands. "I think you two are the perfect pair. One who seeks to save lives and one who seeks to take the lives of the monsters who will not repent. I have complete confidence in you both. I believe you will always find a way. It is your nature."

Irina came back to the table, and we stopped our conversation. There was an awkward silence as she sat, but we were rescued when our waiter came with our entrees and another bottle. We all dug into our meals. This was a top-notch restaurant for a reason.

"This dinner is wonderful. Thank you so much," I said to our host.

He shrugged and refilled everyone's wine glass. "We are celebrating the rebirth of my beautiful Irina and perhaps working together in the future. An excellent meal is a perfect way to begin."

We finished our meal, spoke of the weather, the things Irina was learning, and when all the food was eaten and the wine drunk ... it was time to go. I looked at the big Russian as we stood. "I thank you again for being such a wonderful host. I must regretfully decline your generous job offer. I simply have no desire to encounter another vampire. Not ever."

Kamenev sighed and shrugged. "I understand, Walt. You never chose your birthright or your place in all of this. I thank you for your company and considering my offer." He reached out and gave my hand a warm shake and turned to his daughter.

He held out his arms and gently embraced his beloved Irina. He whispered something to her in Russian and smiled at her as he released her.

She smiled back at him, but her eyes turned toward me. "*Da, Papa*," she agreed quietly.

I'd seen that look in Irina's eyes before. I had a feeling that we were going to have a long talk about this.

CHAPTER 4

"You need to tell me why," she asked as we walked the snowy streets together in the dark. She was still holding my arm but a little tighter.

I took a cold breath of air and let it out slow. I could see the vapor freeze in the air. A cold night that was about to get colder if I didn't tread lightly. "Irina, I killed a lot of people on my last adventure. I have no desire to do that again. It's not who I am. It never was."

"Vampires!" she exclaimed. "*Gryazznyye vampiry*. You should not be ashamed. You should be proud."

I stopped and looked down at her. She only switched to Russian when she was angry. Even frowning at me, she was a vision. "Irina, the first vampire I killed was your mother, and I will feel terrible about that forever. No, it wasn't my fault, but I still did it. I got lucky, or I would have killed you too. I'm done with that."

That seemed to get through. The frown ran

away from her face, and she grabbed my arm, and we started walking again. "You saved me, Walt. You did."

"It was lucky, Irina. I took a terrible chance because you were out of time. Luck was on our side, or I would have been responsible for another death. I would have been the one to kill a beautiful young woman. Don't make me go there again."

I felt her squeeze my arm, and her head leaned on my shoulder. "You make good decisions. You save people. Harada, Kimiko, American soldiers, all of us. Papa wants you to make decisions. He likes you."

I gave the mitten she had placed on my arm a pat. "I like him too. I hated having to refuse the man. There is something amazing about your father. It's easy to talk to him, and you don't want to disappoint him. I just … can't."

She stiffened and squeezed my arm hard. Three figures were walking toward us. One had a black coat and a red scarf. "They are drunk," she explained. "I smell Vodka on breath."

I did a double take and looked at her and the distance of the three men. "You can smell vodka from *that distance?*"

Her face turned into a mask of hate, and she took a step away from me. "That is not all I smell. It is two men, and they are not alone." She spat on the ground. "*Vampiry Walt!*"

The three sauntered up to us. The one with the red scarf and the brutish face was smiling. An equally large man in a battered ski jacket walked beside him. His black hair was long and his beard covered most of his face, except for two mean blue eyes. The bearded one pointed at us. "*Eto oni?*" he growled.

Red scarf nodded. "*Da, eto oni.*"

I stole a quick glance at Irina and didn't like what I saw. She was shaking, and her fists were balled up. She radiated rage, and I wasn't sure she could contain it. I wasn't sure I wanted her to.

The two big men parted, and a smaller figure stepped forward. A large hood hid the face, and clawed hands reached up to pull back the hood. I'd rather he didn't. White eyes and hardly any hair marked the age of the thing. It was a hundred years old, for sure. Male, probably.

It hissed at us and spoke. "*Tvoya krov' sdelayet menya sil'nym.*"

I leaned toward Irina. "What was that?"

She pointed right at the thing. "He say our blood make him strong."

I laughed. "Really? Well, no reason to make him wait." I took out a small pen knife out of my pocket, and the two men took a step back. I held it up so they could see the tiny blade. The thing was a toy. I took the knife and ran it down my left palm, making a long, small cut that welled with blood.

The old vampire hissed, and its tongue came out as if it could taste the blood already. It put a hand on the shoulder of the two men. "*Voz'mi devochku poka ya kormlyu.*"

"Sweetheart ... what is he saying?" I whispered to the woman beside me.

Her voice was like ice. "He says they take me while he feeds on you."

I looked at her and smiled. "Oh, honey. You're not going to let that happen, are you?"

"*Nyet. NYET!*" she screamed, glaring pure murder.

That did it. The two men ran at her while the vampire leapt at me, tongue lolling and clawed hands outstretched. He put his hands on my shoulders and took me to the ground. I smiled at him and shouted, "*Syn Meduzy!*" just before I slapped my bloody palm on his forehead.

He stood up fast and took two steps backward before falling into the snow and screaming as he died. I got up as fast as I could to see how Irina was doing. I needn't have bothered.

I've seen men kicked in the groin before, but I'd never seen a man kicked so hard that he lifted over six feet in the air. The crunch and high-pitched scream the bearded assailant let out as he fell to earth made it clear that the fight was over for him. It was doubtful he would ever be the same.

Irina was standing in front of the brutish lout with the red scarf. The poor fool was looking at his broken partner and did the wrong thing. He reached out and slapped her hard.

Her eyes blazed, and she slapped him back, but her hand was a blur, and I could hear the snap as his neck broke. He crumpled to the ground, dead. That didn't stop Irina from screaming and kicking his body another twenty yards into a brick wall.

I walked toward her and held up both my hands. "It's okay, Irina. It's done. You won, sweetheart. You won."

She was panting, and her hands were flexing into fists. Her eyes were still wild, but she looked at me. I guess that was all she needed. It was incredible to see that volcanic rage just evaporate. Within seconds, she was breathing regularly, and her expressive dark eyes looked in mine. "Okay, Walt."

I placed my right hand on her shoulder while my left dripped blood into the white snow. "You need this ... don't you? To get closure, to finish the fight. Is that what you want, Irina?"

She let out a big sigh, and I saw tears starting to grow. "Da, Walt. I must fight ... *and they must die for what they have done to me!*"

I pulled her to me, careful not to put my bloody palm against her coat, and held her. She wrapped her arms around me and gave me a gentle squeeze. "Okay, Irina. I get it. This is bigger than me. We will help your father, and we will rid the world of vampires. Their time is done."

CHAPTER 5

We didn't talk to each other for the rest of the walk. We got back to the apartment, shed our coats, and collapsed on the sofa. The adrenaline dump left us flat and listless. About ten seconds after we sat down, the phone rang.

Irina looked at me, and we both laughed. "I'll get it. Relax, honey." I got up and picked up the loud old rotary phone. "Hello?" I called into the receiver.

"Walt! Are you two okay?" It was Kamenev checking up on his daughter.

"Yes, my friend. What is your worry?"

I heard laughter on the other end of the phone. "My men found a melted vampire and a couple of broken thugs. I know only one man who could do that to one of those monsters."

"Guilty, Comrade. Irina and I ran into the three fools on the way home. We encountered the one with the red scarf earlier. He was rude to her, and Irina threw him clear across the street."

I could hear Kamenev laughing, and I joined him. "She has her mother's temper, I am afraid."

I shrugged, even though he couldn't see it. "You'd think that after Irina tossed him that far, he would give up. Instead, he came back looking for us ... with reinforcements."

"Da, that vampire was very old. Probably one of the gangsters we have been trying to eliminate for a long time. You have my thanks."

"You are very welcome, Comrade."

There was silence, and I could tell he was searching for words. "There is the matter of the other two. One has smashed genitals and is in for months of medical assistance. The damage is incredible. He cannot even speak. The other ... the other has a broken neck, and every rib is destroyed ... was that ..."

"Yes, that was Irina. It was self-defense. The monster told them to 'take her' while he fed on me."

"*Eti ublyudki!*" I heard him swear.

"I agree. I'm just glad it was us and not someone else they went after. There are more of these things, and their henchmen are spread all around the world, am I right?"

"Da, Walt. On every continent there are monsters who are causing suffering and death. They are hiding, but they are there."

I looked at Irina, and she tilted her head at me,

encouraging me to say what needed to be said. "Mister Kamenev, I'm reconsidering that offer you made at dinner. I think we need to talk about it some more before I can accept. Would that be okay?"

"Yes! Yes, please come by my office tomorrow morning, and I will explain further. I think you are the right man for this position."

"Well … I guess we'll see. Any chance Svetlana can make us tea? Nobody does it better."

I heard the big man let out a belly laugh. "I will tell her you said that. She is sure to make you tea. She has a soft spot for you, I think."

"I'll see you tomorrow, Comrade."

"Good night to you both," he said as he hung up.

I sighed and walked over to the sofa, and sat very close to Irina. I didn't look at her as I spoke. "We are to visit your father tomorrow morning at his office. He wants to tell us more about what we would be doing. Okay?"

She snuggled into me and let out her own sigh. "Okay, Walt. I love you."

"I love you too. Do you want me to light a fire?"

"*Da*, a fire is nice."

I got up and started moving the wood and kindling. "I really don't want to do this, you know."

"It has to be done, Walt."

I stopped making the fire and looked at her. "I know, Irina. I know."

CHAPTER 6

The ancient elevator looked like a cage, and it creaked and complained all the way up to the top floor. "I hate this thing," I chuckled to Irina. She just smiled and squeezed my hand. I grit my teeth as the bones of my hands protested, and I almost yelped. She was still getting used to this newfound strength. I didn't have the heart to tell her she hurt me.

We got off the old metal deathtrap and walked down the ornate, antique rug to a large desk. A woman in a blue pantsuit and a red star on her lapel was reading something and writing on a piece of paper. Her glasses were thick-rimmed, and her hair was pulled back into a severe-looking ponytail. She frowned as she worked.

"Hello, Svetlana!" I called down the hall.

Her head jerked up, and that sour expression disappeared, replaced by a grin. She jumped out of her chair and ran to us with her arms outstretched. Surprisingly, Irina opened her arms and grinned, too. I didn't get it, but that was okay.

After their embrace ended, Svetlana looked at me, grabbed my shoulders, and kissed me on each cheek. I stole a glance at Irina to be sure she wouldn't rip Svetlana's head off in a fit of jealous rage. Nope. She was fine with it. This whole thing was very Russian.

The older woman put her hand under my chin and turned my face, inspecting it. "Walt, you have lost weight. We must fatten you up." She looked over her glasses at me and gave me a wicked smile. "I will make tea and bring treats."

I laughed. "Not sure Mister Kamenev wants me chubby for my new job. But ... some of your amazing tea would go a long way. Thanks, Svetlana. You're the best."

She gave me a light slap on the cheek. "You flatter me. Go see Ivan. He is excited to talk with you."

I heard Irina giggle beside me, and I laughed, too. Svetlana marched away from us and left us to find our way. Why not? We knew this office like the back of our hand. We continued down the broad corridor and went around the corner to see Kamenev sitting at his desk.

The older man was all business in his crisp blue suit. He noticed us right away and whipped off his reading glasses, standing tall with his arms out. "My darling, Walt! Please come in. Sit, sit." he added while gesturing to the two comfortable chairs in front of his vast desk.

We sat, and the big man let out a big sigh as he planted himself in his leather chair. "Ah, so you have reconsidered my offer?"

I looked at Irina, and she nodded at me to talk. We were good that way. "I'm not completely agreed, but I do see the merits of what you are proposing. I just need to know what is expected of me, of us."

The big Russian tented his fingers on his desk. "I understand completely. You want to know what will happen. Where you will be going and what you will be doing. Yes?"

I nodded and looked at Irina. She did the same.

"Very well," he said and sat back. "I envision you both as a response team. Someone we can call specifically to deal with vampires when the need arises."

I raised an eyebrow. "When you say, 'deal,' why do I think you mean kill?"

He shrugged, "If need be. If you can find another solution that is acceptable, that would be wonderful."

"Why us?"

Kamenev laughed. "Who better? You must understand that for the vampires, you are the ... how you say? The 'boogeyman.' Yes, that's it. They know what you represent, and they fear you. Ultimately, they must respect your ability."

I frowned. "You actually think they will listen to me?"

"*Pochemu da!*" he exclaimed. "Every single one of these fiends know the legend. They know who you are, and after the skirmish in Japan, they know what you can do. That will definitely command their attention."

I patted my leg with one hand while I thought. "And Irina, she will help me find them?"

His eyes darted to his daughter, and he looked at her as he answered. "Among other things. She is to be your muscle. I think that is the term in English."

"Nobody better," I laughed, looking at the petite killing machine to my right. She beamed and took my hand. "What would life be like for us?" I asked.

"You would be busy. You would be charged with the responsibility of finding vampires, bringing them in, or destroying them."

"In Russia?"

"*Da*, definitely Russia. However, we would ask you to travel to other places in the world that would need your specific skill set."

I looked over at Irina. "Would you like that? Would you like to see other places in the world?

"*Da*, Walt," she answered, giving my hand a light squeeze. "I would like that very much."

I took a long breath and let it out. "It would seem

the decision has been made. I want to save vampires, Irina wants to kill them, and the world would be happy with either solution. Everybody wins."

"You are a smart boy," Kamenev said with a chuckle. "We will start your training tomorrow."

"Are the two of us going to be enough?"

My Russian friend smirked at me. "No. I have a few other members of the team. They have already agreed to participate."

"Oh, good. Backup is good."

He stood up and grinned, "We have recruited excellent members to work with you. The very best."

"Good to hear. Will we like them?"

He thumped his desk with one hand. "Definitely. They are old friends of yours, Walt."

CHAPTER 7

Names on a piece of paper can mean so much. The paper I was holding made me smile. "You're joking!" I laughed as I read the names.

"You approve?" Kamenev said with a gleam in his eye.

"I do, you know I do. These people expect me to lead?"

"Walt, each member of the team jumped at the chance to work with you. This is a surprise?"

"Uh … yes. I mean, these people have a lot more experience and education than I do."

Kamenev held up a finger. "Ah, but you have something that they do not."

I narrowed my eyes as I stared at him. "And that is?"

He gave me a mischievous grin. "Magic."

All three of us laughed. We all knew magic had nothing to do with it. The science wasn't completely settled, but it certainly wasn't magic.

When we were done laughing, I looked at the big Russian bear and asked a question. "Okay, we're in. What happens now?"

"Now? Now you go home. Eat, relax, rest. Tomorrow, it begins." He reached in his desk drawer and handed us a piece of paper. "Irina can help you find the address. Be there at nine in the morning to begin training."

"Both of us?"

"*Da*, both of you. After training, we will dine again at Café Pushkin. This time, the Fireplace Hall to meet the team." He reached under the desk and brought out a familiar black case. "You left this in Japan. Oyabun insisted that I return it to you."

I opened it and saw the mace engraved with Medusa's Son in many languages. It had been cleaned and polished to a shine. The weapon made just for me that used my blood to finish any vampire stupid enough to get close.

I took the case with a smile and raised an eyebrow at the old Russian. "Café Pushkin? The Fireplace Hall? Difficult reservations to get. Was that Uncle Yuri?"

He grinned, and his eyes were steel. "No. I made these reservations a week ago."

****

Irina and I walked in silence, the black case under my arm. I looked at her and said, "So we're doing this?

You know it could change everything."

"Not everything," she answered with a smile. "You and me together. That is all that matters."

I smiled in spite of myself. "My darling, Irina. Will you feel the same way when the bodies start to pile up? Will I?"

She looked ahead as we walked. "There is nobody better than my father at planning. He is a man who gets things done. So are you."

I threw an arm over her slender shoulders. "I'm not going to lie. Having you by my side gives me a lot of confidence."

She smiled and gave me a playful punch in the ribs. "You like having strong woman?"

I laughed. "Yeah! You can do all the fighting, and I'll never have to open a tough pickle jar again."

She stopped walking and looked up at me, frowning. "What is pickle jar, and why must it open?"

CHAPTER 8

We got to the address just before nine in the morning. It was underwhelming. A grey brick, run-down old building covered in pigeon droppings, and some of the windows were boarded up. Others had nothing at all. No glass, nothing. There were two big doors at the entrance that were covered in dirt and patches of rust.

I scowled at the wreck of the building. "You sure this is right?"

Irina walked past me, up the stairs, and beckoned me to follow. "This is the right address, and my father does not make mistakes. Come, Walt."

She easily opened the huge, heavy front doors, and the hinges moaned as it swung wide. We stepped into the gloom, and it took a moment for my eyes to adjust. Not Irina. She had walked right up to a soldier standing in a shadow. He was dressed in black with an AK-47 strapped over his shoulder. He didn't blink as he looked at us.

"*Kto ty?*" Irina asked.

"*Spetsnaz*," he answered.

Russian special forces? Well, this was getting interesting. His eyes moved to me. "Baranov?"

I nodded.

"Follow me," he offered with a thick accent. He turned and walked through the monstrous old building until he found a plain set of stairs that went down. He led us downstairs and we walked into a vast room that was the basement. A cement floor and walls surrounded us, and equipment was scattered around the room. There were punching bags on chains, mats for wrestling, and targets at the end of a hall that looked like a shooting range. Grotesque martial-arts dummies with scowling faces were on the edges of the mats, and a primitive-looking weight room was in one corner.

Four people stood on the mats, looking at us. Three of them wore identical navy tracksuits, and one old man was wearing a long white coat with a high collar. The man in the coat was smiling. Nobody else was.

There was a tough-looking older man with tattoos on his neck. Tall, grey, and mean. His eyes narrowed as he looked us over.

A woman with blonde hair cut into a short but feminine style glared at us with cold, blue eyes. Her body was toned, and she didn't look like she had smiled in a decade. A young man, perhaps a little older than me, was glaring our way. He had very short, black hair and an equally dark beard. His stygian eyes were cold.

I shrugged and spoke up. "Baranov. Here for training."

The old man in the white smock smiled and held up some clippers. "I am Anatoly. I am here for haircut."

****

I was sitting in a chair, getting my hair cut, and I could feel my long, light-brown locks falling onto my arms and shoulders. I was part of a special force now. I hated to admit it, but hair that can be grabbed by a vampire is a bad idea. My hair didn't have the DNA strand anywhere but the roots. It served no purpose. This was a better idea.

While Anatoly was shearing me, I could see Irina working with the woman at the target range. Her name was Darya and she didn't say much. My lady love was learning how to use an amazing weapon. A tactical crossbow that could shoot five bolts. You just had to push on a lever to reload the beast. I could hear the bolts hit the target with a loud *thwack*.

When my cut was done, I ran my hand over my head and felt that my hair was not quite as short as the Spetsnaz who were here to train us. I thanked Anatoly, and the old man gave me a quick bow and walked out of the place. That left me looking at the two men here to train me. "Well, what's next?" I asked.

The older man stepped forward and had some padded headgear in his hands. "You will train in hand-to-hand combat." His English was quite good. "I am Oleg. I will teach you to use mace." He gestured with his head to the younger man with the black hair and beard. "Sergei will teach you to fight with hands."

I smiled. "Good. If I'm going to do this, I need to have more options than bleeding all over anyone attacking me."

CHAPTER 9

It started out easy enough. Sergei and Oleg fit me with the headgear. It was like wearing a tight leather pillow on my head. It felt weird with my newly shorn hair, but it would protect me. I only have one brain.

Oleg put small pads on his hands and came to stand in front of me. My hands were sweating. They always did that when I was amped up and putting on the gear, and seeing Oleg in front of me got my heart pumping.

"Today, you learn how to protect yourself from hit," Sergei explained. He stood beside me and brought his fists up to his cheeks. "Hands up to protect face, *Da?*"

I did as commanded and balled my fists, bringing them just below my eyes so I could still see. "Like this?" I asked.

"*Da*, hands up for face, but bring elbows down for belly." Sergei showed me what he wanted.

Keeping my hands where they needed to be, I

dropped my elbows. It felt a little awkward, but it was a smart way to stand in a fight, like a shell, to keep me protected.

Sergei didn't smile, but he did give a slight nod of the head. Barely detectable, but there. "Today, you must always come back to that position. No matter what."

"That's all?"

Sergei looked at Oleg, and the big old fighter stepped forward. Uh oh. He held up the pads and took a step even closer. Was I supposed to hit them or something?

I was just about to ask when Oleg jabbed at me with a left. It was slow, and I was able to duck, but I felt it touch the leather headgear.

"*Nyet*! Back away or block!" Sergei barked. "Your dodge was clumsy and too large a movement. Hands back to face."

I did as he commanded, and Oleg stepped forward again. He threw two strikes. These were faster. I blocked the first and backed out of range for the second. Definitely a win. Sergei didn't say anything, and I took that as a good sign.

We continued like this for a couple of minutes. A couple of very long minutes. My arms and shoulders were burning, and my hands felt like cement boulders. Keeping them up got harder and harder.

Eventually, Sergei called a stop to our lesson. "You are getting better, but we still have a long way to go." He stopped talking when he saw we had a visitor. Ivan Kamenev had slowly slipped into this hidden Spetsnaz dungeon. He gave a small wave to us and turned his head to look at his daughter.

There was another loud smack as a crossbow bolt connected with the target. I could see the grouping around the bullseye. She was good and getting better. She turned after she shot and smiled at her father.

Sergei took the pads from Oleg and threw them into a corner. "Very good. Enough for today. You will work with Oleg on how to hold and use the mace. He is expert on medieval weaponry."

I took off the headgear and wiped some sweat off my forehead. "Okay, what is Irina doing?"

He shrugged. "Working with Darya, hand to hand combat."

"Really?" I asked and looked at the floor. Oh crap! "Uh, Sergei … I'd hold off on that. She doesn't know her own strength yet. Maybe weights would be better?"

He scowled at me and walked right into my personal space. "You may be '*Syn Meduzy*,' but you do not tell me my business. We are experts, and you are here to listen to us."

I smiled at him. "You are completely right. But

let me tell you something, comrade. I've watched that little beauty break a man's neck with a slap of her hand and then kick him over twenty feet. It's up to you. If she punches a hole clean through Darya's head, well … you were warned. She is NOT what she looks like."

Sergei squinted at me, reading my face. He curled a lip and shook his head slowly, not looking at me. "Maybe you are right. Weights are good start as well."

I smiled at him. "Thank you for listening, Sergei. Would you come with me for a second?" I started walking toward Kamenev and gestured for the young Russian to follow me. He shrugged and came along.

Kamenev held out a hand. "Walt, you are sweating and learning. Is there anything better?"

I laughed as I took his hand. "It is pretty cool and I do have a lot to learn. Listen, are there any spots available on the team you are putting together?"

He nodded slowly. "We can add more. Do you have someone in mind?"

"Yes, I do." I gestured with my thumb at Sergei, who was just behind me. "This guy, Sergei. I think he's perfect for our team."

CHAPTER 10

Kamenev shrugged. "May I ask why? Why do you want this man with us?"

I looked at Sergei and smiled. "He's tough, he tells the truth, and he listens. He's willing to consider the impossible and make the smart choice. Considering what we're facing, I think he's just the man for the job."

We both looked at Sergei, who was considering the offer. He frowned and gave us a short nod. "I think I would like this assignment. I have never seen these creatures, and I do not like that they feed on others. I would see them stopped or dead."

"Very good," Kamenev said. "I will make the arrangements."

Sergei smiled, saluted, and walked over to the two women working on Irina's crossbow skills. They had a brief conversation, and I saw Darya turn to Irina and steer towards the weights. Now, this I wanted to see, but Oleg had other plans.

The big medieval arms expert called me over

to a corner of the dark, damp basement, where there was an assortment of black metal weapons in a pile. He fished out a mace that wasn't too different from the one I'd been given in Japan, but what surprised me was when he pulled out a small shield. He handed me both and found similar weapons for himself.

He waited until I had the shield attached and then did the same. "Shield must always be ready, always between you and enemy. Lift it higher."

My poor shoulder ached, but I did lift it as instructed. "Like this?"

"*Da*. Now I will hit. Be ready."

The big Russian grit his teeth and swung the mace behind him and over the top, coming down hard on the shield. Pain ran up my arm, and I almost dropped the shield.

"Good! You can lift shield higher to take hit sooner. It will be less." Oleg wound up again, and I decided to see If he was right. I grunted and lifted the shield, and it was less of a blow. Probably because the head of his mace was not moving as fast when it hit my shield.

"Your turn," Oleg said, lifting his own wooden shield. "Swing back, hit shield."

I did as he instructed, and as soon as I started moving the mace, I realized it was a good deal heavier than the modern version I was used to. Still, I got it moving and brought it down with a thump on Oleg's shield.

"Good, but do not drop your own shield when you strike mine. Do again."

I knew he was right, so I repeated the action, concentrating on keeping the shield still while the mace moved. It was harder, but I could see the value in protecting myself while I smacked an enemy.

We were interrupted by Darya coming over and saying something to Oleg, and he did a double take. Sergei walked up to us, and his face was a picture. "You need to see this to believe it."

Making our way to the weight area, we saw Irina laying on a bench, pushing a bar with stacks of steel on each side. She was concentrating on what she was doing but easily moved the bar up and down.

"She has never lifted weights before, and she is playing with four hundred pounds," Darya whispered to us.

Sergei put a hand on my shoulder. "It was good that you warned me about this. I am sorry for the way I spoke to you."

"Don't be. You were right. It's not for me to tell you your business, and I really am here to learn. What you're teaching could save my life. I just wanted you to know what you were dealing with."

Irina racked it easily and looked back at us.

"Should I lift more?"

"We don't have more," Oleg said with a shake of his head. "I will have more plates for the bars sent to us tomorrow."

I let out a sigh. "We're doing this again tomorrow? Same time?"

"*Da*, same time," Sergei confirmed. "We have done enough for today. Rest well tonight, and we will show you new things in the morning."

I looked at the young Russian. "You're the boss, Sergei, but I do have one piece of advice. Don't let Irina hit anything that is alive."

Sergei looked at the pretty, slender brunette sitting on the bench and smiling at us. "She doesn't hit anything but a punching bag."

I walked over to Irina and opened my arms wide. She pulled me into a tight hug. So strong! I looked at the three trainers looking at us. "Might want to get a few more punching bags in here. You know, just in case."

CHAPTER 11

After a long walk home and a long shower, we cuddled on the sofa, watching the fire. "You're pretty good with a crossbow," I said.

"*Da*, I like crossbow."

"I wonder why they aren't training you to use a gun."

She looked up at me and wrinkled her nose. "I don't like gun. Loud and bad smell."

"Of course! Those enhanced senses of yours would not enjoy the noise and the cordite. I can't help thinking there's more to it, though. They gave you a crossbow for a reason."

I felt her shrug. "It is easy to see target and put arrow in the circle. Not hard."

"I think you have a lot to learn about what your new body can do."

She snuggled closer, and I heard a change in her voice. "I am scared sometimes that I will hurt you, Walt."

Her head was against my shoulder, so I couldn't see her face, but it sounded like she was tearing up. This girl had demons, and they were back. She needed to talk this out.

"Okay, let's look at that. Ever since you changed back, you have never hurt me."

"I have not?"

"No. You came close a couple of times, but that's to be expected. You're getting better and better."

"Really?"

"Yes, and I have more good news."

"Tell me, Walt."

"When you're training, you're going to be able to use your strength. All of it! That's going to help you learn what is full strength and what is not. You'll be able to measure your power."

"You think?"

"I really do. Just promise me one thing, Irina."

"Anything."

I took a moment to gather my thoughts. "Promise me you won't let your full power out when you're training with a person. When you're punching or hacking at a thing, let it out. But never against something that is a living person."

"Of course, But vampires are okay?"

"If it's a fight, and you have to, do it. Everything you've got."

She moved away from me so we could see each other's faces. Her eyes were watery. "Thank you, Walt. You understand me."

"I do. More than most. I think you are a miracle, Irina. That you can do what you do. That you're even alive. It's amazing."

She answered with a quick kiss on the lips. "I love you," she whispered.

"I love you too, and that's what's going to get us through this madness." I stretched. "Speaking of madness, we should get some sleep. Who knows what they'll have us doing tomorrow."

****

We made it to the basement of the old building, and our trainers were waiting. I saw a stack of new plates for Irina to toss around near the weights, and Sergei took my advice on the punching bags. I saw five new ones laying against the far wall. Smart guy.

We started with me on the weights, with Darya supervising and Irina working with Sergei. There was a big part of me that wanted to remind Irina of her promise, but that wasn't necessary. She would remember.

I wanted to watch Irina do her thing, but I was too busy sucking at pumping iron. The first thing Darya had me do was bench press. It felt, wrong. It was a long bar with only a few small plates on each side. It felt like

I was fighting to keep the bar in position when I should have been concentrating on moving it properly. I felt weak, and it wasn't long until Darya called a stop to my pathetic efforts.

"One hundred and thirty pounds." She deadpanned. "You have not lifted before, have you?"

"Never. It's all I can do to lift my carcass out of bed in the morning. Sorry, Darya. Not a lot of natural ability to work with."

She tilted her head to one side. "*Da*, this is true. But it will make any improvement seem large."

"That's the spirit!" I cheered weakly.

I heard a low, hollow noise, and I looked over to see Irina standing on a pile of wooden boxes. They were getting her to jump higher and higher, stacking the boxes to make it harder. She'd just jumped to the top of two of the boxes. She looked at me and smiled.

I gave her a thumbs-up and turned my attention back to Darya. "What's next?"

"Deadlifts."

A one-word answer that filled me with dread. Anything that had the word "dead" in it couldn't be good. She walked me over to a rusty old Olympic bar with a forty-five-pound plate on each side. She grabbed the bar with a wide grip, bent at the knees, bringing her rear end low, and stood up with the bar. "Easy," she announced and let the bar fall to the ground.

"Right, easy," I laughed and stepped up to the bar. I got a wide grip and heaved it up.

"Use legs, not back," Darya commanded.

I tried it her way, and it was better. "How many?" I asked between gritted teeth.

"As many as you can do," she barked over the noise of my grunting.

Great. There was a rhythm to the thump as I plopped it down and picked it up. I got to twenty, and my legs were on fire. It felt like a piano wire was stretched from my butt to the back of my knee.

"Not bad start," Darya said.

There was a loud thump and I looked over to see Irina standing on a pile of boxes almost as tall as Sergei. The Russian was standing there with his eyes wide, shaking his head. Irina was grinning and waving at me like a little girl.

Sergei walked up to me and leaned closer to whisper in my ear. "She just jumped to a stack of boxes six feet high, and it was easy for her."

I laughed, "You think she can go higher?"

He shrugged and whispered again. "Don't know. We don't have higher. We have never needed more boxes."

I looked over at the slender dynamo and she was laughing. I looked at Sergei and shrugged. "You can whisper if you want, but I can tell you that she heard every word."

He snapped his head to look at Irina, who just nodded her head.

CHAPTER 12

Oleg was staring at Irina, who was still giggling and standing on top of the stack of wooden boxes. He walked over to me, and he was carrying a pair of small wooden shields. "Time to learn to hit with these."

The big Russian handed me one of the two shields and beckoned for me to follow him to the punching bags. He showed me how to use my body behind the shield and hit it with a body check and a backhanded version.

I hit the bag with the shield and found it wasn't as easy as Oleg made it look. Still, the bag was moving, and there was a good sound. I was getting better.

Sergei came over with Irina and started working on a bag about twenty feet from us. Jabs and crosses were the strikes she was being taught. Sergei was giving his instructions in Russian, but it was pretty much the same as he taught me. Hands at the cheeks, elbows down, and he was making her hit the bag.

Irina was doing a good job keeping her hands

up, but the big difference between us was the incredible sound when she connected with the large punching bag. The chain holding the bag would strain, and the foundations of the building shook with every strike.

"*Sil'neye!*" Sergei yelled at her. "*SIL'NEYE!*"

Irina screamed and threw a right hand that ripped the bag where the straps attached to the chains, and it sailed into the wall. Irina stood there, blinking and looking at the bag. "Sorry," she murmured.

Sergei looked at me, and we both broke up laughing. Darya and Oleg joined in. Irina eventually chuckled at the situation as well.

I put a hand on the striking instructor's shoulder. "You are a great teacher, Sergei."

"*Spasibo,*" he answered with a grin.

We stopped laughing as Kamenev came into view with his impeccable blue suit and two bodyguards. He was smiling. "Progress is good to see. Tell me what has been accomplished."

Sergei stood and started talking in Russian. Kamenev held a hand to stop him and pointed at me. He nodded and apologized. "Sorry, Walt." He turned back to Kamenev and explained. "We have been working on their hand-to-hand skills, as well as their proficiency with the weapons you requested. Irina is hitting everything she wants with her tactical crossbow. Walt is progressing nicely with shield and mace."

Darya stepped up. "The young man is improving his form, but his strength still needs time to develop. Irina ..." She looked at the ground and shook her head slowly. "The girl has superhuman strength and agility. I have never seen anything like it."

Kamenev nodded and linked his hands behind his back. "This is good. More time is needed to ready them for the task at hand. Two more weeks of intense training and we will be able to start our work."

"That's it?" I asked, stretching my back. "I think I need more time than that."

The Russian official shrugged. "That is all the time I can give you. It must be remembered that the vampires are still out there, and people are suffering. How long can they wait for our help?"

The man had a point. I sighed, "I guess we should get back to work." I looked at the three trainers. "Weights, fists, or weapons?"

Kamenev laughed. "I believe you are finished for this day. My purpose in coming is to ask you to attend a dinner meeting tonight."

"Café Pushkin?" I asked.

"*Da*, the Fireplace Hall this time."

"Right." I looked at the three trainers and back at the big man. "Would it be possible to invite our trainers? I mean, Sergei is on the team anyway. But

Oleg and Darya have been amazing. I'll be happy to pay for any additional expense if they attend."

Kamenev looked at the three trainers whose eyes widened at the prospect of eating at such an establishment. Everybody in Russia knew of Café Pushkin. Everybody. "It was going to be a meeting of the team only. But, as you say, Sergei is a member of the new division, and it would be helpful if Darya and Oleg knew what was to come. It may guide their training." He clapped his hands together. "*Da*, the state will be happy to pay for their meal. We will eat, drink, and discuss many things. I doubt the Fireplace Hall will ever see such a meeting again!"

CHAPTER 13

Irina and I walked the streets again. Not far from where we took apart those three villains who sought to do us harm. But there was no thought of that. Too many good things on the go tonight for any bad memories. We were making new ones.

After our training, Irina insisted that we stop and dress appropriately for such a dinner. It wasn't like me to dress up, but I would do it for Kamenev. I would do it for her. We found a store for formal men's wear, and I got a nice dark grey suit off the rack. Black shoes, a white shirt, and a black tie later, I was done.

Irina took a little longer. We found a nice store with dresses, and she almost ran into the place. The saleswomen were a little cold to this young woman, but when I showed them some cash, things soon turned around. After a few unsuccessful attempts, she found the perfect dress. It was a shimmering silver on the upper part of the dress, but her shoulders and arms were bare. From the waist down, there were silver icicles that reached into the black, pleated skirt. Shoes were easy as she liked a low heel and black shoes were plentiful.

There was a bit of an argument when I told her what else was needed to complete her look. But, this time ... I was the one to get my way. We stopped at a jeweler, and I was able to get her a beautiful silver necklace and matching earrings. She didn't want such an extravagance, but her eyes lit up when she tried it all on. Her smile was so endearing.

We were all polished, and it felt good to walk to the line of the famous restaurant dressed to kill. People stared again, but it was at a couple who were well-dressed. Irina's dress gleamed beneath her open coat, and her silver earrings and matching necklace looked amazing as they caught the light. Her hair was in a long braid that went to the middle of her back. Neat and elegant.

My new haircut worked with the suit and tie. The Maître De looked us up and down but quickly recognized the lovely Ms. Kamenev. He learned fast. You had to give him that. "Miss Kamenev, *tebya ozhidayut*." He looked at me and gave me the same smarmy smile. "Comrade Baranov, no?"

I nodded, and he gestured for us to follow him. I felt Irina squeeze my arm. We were both excited to see this special part of the famed restaurant. It did not disappoint. We walked through wide, glass doors into a room like no other. A gentle light from the spectacular crystal chandeliers above us showed the incredible décor. Large, white pillars that were topped in gold trim reached from the floor to the roof. A massive old fireplace dominated one end of the room. It had white tiles above it, and there was an ornate white and gold mantle surrounding the roaring fire.

Tables with dark green tablecloths and white candelabras were pushed together to make one vast table. There were wooden chairs with red cushions surrounding the table, and it was set for ten guests. Most were already here, and they were all familiar faces.

Kamenev sat at the head of the table, of course, and stood when he saw us. The other guests looked our way and moved to stand and greet us.

The first to get to us was a well-groomed Japanese man in a black suit. He had tattoos that poked out from the bottom of his white cuffs. He was Yakuza, part of that frightening Japanese underground. He was a friend.

"Harada!" I laughed when I saw him. A handshake wasn't needed. A smile broke across his serious countenance, and we grabbed each other in a bear hug. "So good to see you, my friend."

"*Hai*," he grunted. Never was a talker.

"I'm so glad you are with us. A noble warrior is always good to have." He smiled, nodded, and moved to greet Irina. This made room for the next guest to move closer.

She was wearing an elegant ivory dress that showed off her slender frame. Gold earrings were shining in her black shoulder-length hair. That wry smirk was on her face and I thought I saw some tears behind the black-rimmed glasses.

"Doctor Kimiko!" I said, tearing up myself.

"Walt," she barely got out as she came to me and gave me the gentlest of hugs. "I like your haircut," she said.

I laughed and backed up, holding her at arm's length. "You look fantastic! I think living in San Francisco agrees with you."

She grinned at me. "It does. Thank you for that, Walt."

I raised an eyebrow. "Thanks for what? I didn't do anything."

Kimiko brought her hand up to my chin and gave it a playful shove. "You know very well what I'm talking about. I'm grateful."

I grinned and turned to look at our next guest. He was in an American military uniform. His teeth were white against his very dark skin as he smiled back. There were a few medals on his chest, and I narrowed my eyes when I saw him. "Hey, I know you. Shaw, right? Is that really you?"

"Travis Shaw. He said, "Last time we met was during a messy skirmish in Japan's South Alps. Pretty sure you saved me and two of my men."

"I remember it different. Like you were the ones who came to our rescue."

"Then you remember it wrong, fella!" Shaw said with a laugh. I laughed, too. I'd seen him in action, and he was tough, brave, and had a heart.

"Why are you in this? What made you join up?" I asked, searching his face.

He put his hands on his hips and looked at the ground. "I'll never forget seeing those things storming the roof of the facility. Knowing they are out there, and that they are feeding on people ... that needs to stop." He looked me in the eye and grinned. "Part of me wants to see you melt one of those things again. That's magic, man."

We laughed again, and I turned to the dinner guests I hadn't spoken to. Oleg and Sergei were dressed in suits with turtlenecks. Simple and elegant. We shook hands and smiled at each other. Even though we were back at it tomorrow, we had a great meal in front of us.

The big winner of this occasion had to be Darya. The stern looking taskmaster had completely transformed. She wore a lovely blue dress that brought out her eyes. It was off the shoulders and showed off her toned deltoids. Her serious demeanor was gone, and with a little makeup and a big smile, she looked great.

"Darya! So nice of you to join us. I'm very grateful for your torture sessions, and I'm going to need more."

Her eyes danced as she laughed. "*Da*, thank you for making this possible, Walt." I had to remember that she probably had never eaten at this restaurant. She probably thought she never would.

"It was Comrade Kamenev that has made all this possible. I just thought you deserved a nice meal."

"*Spasibo*," she said and shook my hand with both of hers.

We parted, and I walked to the head of the table. Kamenev was standing and greeted us. He shook my hand, as was his custom. "I am looking forward to this dinner, my friend."

"As am I. There's sure to be some interesting conversation and a great meal."

He leaned in so nobody else could hear him. "Inviting your trainers here was a stroke of genius. They are sure to do a better job and be more invested when they know your mission. You have won them over."

"I just thought it would be a nice way to repay

them for their efforts. Nothing more."

"I wonder, Walt," Kamenev said with a gleam in his eye. "I wonder." He turned to the people standing and talking to each other and tapped a fork on a glass. "My friends, let us sit and dine and talk of things to come."

Everyone smiled and started moving to sit. I found Irina and steered her to the seat closer to her father, who sat at the head of the table, naturally.

I sat beside Irina, and I watched the others take positions around the table. Harada sat beside Kimiko, and the Russians sat together. Shaw took the other end of the table. Waiters came in and filled every glass with a deep red wine.

Kamenev lifted his glass. "A toast to you, my friends. The very first meeting of the Medusa Division."

CHAPTER 14

There were smiles all around as the name of the group was revealed. I winced at the reference but was happy to sip my wine. It was magnificent.

The waiters came and took everyone's order for appetizers and entrees. Irina helped me pick something different from our last visit. When everyone had selected their meals, the waiters left, and Kamenev spoke up. "Everyone in this room is sworn to secrecy on this matter. While it seems self-evident, it must be said, yes?"

Every head nodded in agreement and understanding.

"Good. Very good," he continued. "Here is what we are envisioning. Vampires still exist and cause suffering in the world. Not everyone has the weaponry or expertise to deal with these things. Sometimes, it is a matter of finding these monsters. There are sure to be situations where there is a unique vampire issue that local law enforcement simply cannot solve. That is where the Medusa Division would step in."

"Anywhere?" Shaw asked from the other end of the table.

"*Da,* anywhere who seeks out our help," Kamenev explained. "Such a team must have individuals who have specific and essential roles to be effective." He gestured with his hand back to Shaw and then Sergei. "We have asked Mister Shaw to provide firepower when the need arises. He will be working with Sergei Agapov in this regard."

"Happy to help," Shaw said, lifting a glass to his host and the Russian soldier. Sergei lifted his glass as well.

Kamenev returned the gesture and took a sip. He set the glass down and looked at our friends from Japan. "Harada will also provide firepower and give us the fight we need. He has the additional responsibility of protecting Doctor Kimiko as she performs her duties."

Harada nodded and looked at the doctor sitting beside him. I glanced at the doctor and sent her a wink. She shook her head with a smirk.

The waiters came into the room and started distributing appetizers in front of the different guests. I noticed that they were very careful to ensure that Kamenev and his daughter were the first to be served. Still, more evidence that the man mattered. He mattered a lot.

When everyone was served, Kamenev spoke up again. "Eat, and I will explain more." He shoveled some of his own appetizer into his mouth and swallowed it down. "Doctor Kimiko will be providing assistance with weaponry and treatment for any vampires who seek this help. She is our scientist and expert on these creatures."

The Doctor sat up and looked down the table at the soldiers. "We have been developing ammunition that contains Mister Baranov's DNA. It is housed in a polymer shell and releases after penetrating just below the skin. The effects are immediate and catastrophic for any vampire who is hit by these bullets."

"Pardon me, Doctor." Shaw interrupted. "I've seen firsthand what Walt's DNA does to these things, and it really is fast. But the last time I used some of your magic bullets, they were in an automatic pistol. Do we have other options? Something more powerful?"

The doctor nodded. "Yes, we can make these bullets in a wide variety of calibers. You and Comrade Agapov should decide what weapons would be best. You must keep in mind that you will be carrying normal ammunition as well as the 'magic bullets' you describe. Carrying that much ammunition will limit the number of weapons you can use. I recommend you talk to each other and choose wisely. Inform me of your choice, and I will have our lab in Japan make the ammunition you need."

Shaw and Sergei locked eyes and smiled at each other. They were both looking forward to that conversation and were already communicating. This bode well.

"Will you be joining us on our missions, Doctor?" I asked.

"Sometimes. I will be splitting my time between the labs in San Francisco and Japan. But I will be working with our Russian friends to create a mobile lab that I can use when I accompany you. I will treat any vampires who cooperate when I am there, and I will develop a kit you can use when I am not."

"Bullets are not the only weapons the good doctor has been helping us to develop," Kamenev mentioned from the head of the table.

"No, we have also developed a special crossbow bolt for Irina," the doctor explained. "It has a sharp metal point, but there is a space in the middle that holds a glass vial. Almost like a tiny hourglass. Walt's DNA is in this small glass container at the tip."

"That is a weapon that is deadly to humans or vampires," Sergei observed.

Kimiko looked his way. "That is correct. It is also a silent weapon with a decent range. Between the firepower that you provide and the stealth that Irina's weapon brings, this gives the team a lot of flexibility."

Kamenev held up a hand when the waiters returned to remove our empty plates and deliver our entrees. When we had the room, he pointed at me with a fork and started cutting his steak. "And now we come to the last. The role of Baranov and his lady love."

Irina reached out and took my hand. I looked at her and smiled.

"My daughter has superior strength and senses. It is her duty to find these creatures and if Walt is threatened, dispatch them. She is there to protect the entire team, but Walt is the priority. I have no doubt in her ability to defend or kill."

"*Da*, Papa. I can do this. I will not fail." Irina answered with a small voice.

Kamenev winked at her. "The vampires are terrified of 'Syn Meduzy' or the legend of Medusa's Son. A man who can kill them with a touch," he explained.

Shaw chuckled and smiled at me. "Not so much a legend as they thought. I've seen it firsthand."

Kamenev laughed, too, and shook his head. "I will never forget the day I saw Walt's blood melt the creature that attacked my family." He looked at Irina with soft eyes. "And I will never forget the day he brought my daughter back to me."

Doctor Kimiko put her elbows on the table.

"This legend is worldwide. It is a story or prophecy that the end of the vampire nation will come with the arrival of the one they call 'Medusa's Son.' Do not underestimate the psychological power this gives us. When they know who is standing in front of them, they will be less likely to attack and more likely to listen."

"And this is the point," Kamenev continued. "It is Walt's duty to lead this team into the mission and get the vampires to comply or destroy them."

"Sounds straightforward enough," Shaw said and shoveled some food in his mouth.

Kamenev shook his head. "I doubt that. The fiends have paid off ordinary people to look after their interests, and you will never know how they will react. I can tell you that the older the vampire, the less likely they will cooperate. It won't be easy to find them, and you will be walking in blind. Every single time."

It was my turn to talk. "Look, I'm going to be completely honest with you. If we were a team of assassins, this would be easy. Find 'em and kill 'em. Game over. But I'm always going to try and get them to submit to treatment. I know there is a shred of humanity in there, and I will always try to reach that and save them."

"Sounds risky," Sergei observed.

"It is," I agreed. "But that's the deal. Irina and I lead the way, you guys provide backup, and the doctor helps anyone we can bring to her. We're going to make some tough choices along the way. I will always listen to you, so don't be afraid to speak your mind."

"Walt will have the final decision in all matters," Kamenev announced. "I know he will listen to you. It is his nature. But always understand that he has the last say. Agreed?"

The dinner guests looked at each other, and each one nodded their head in agreement.

Kamenev smiled and looked at the three trainers sitting together. 'That gives you two weeks to get them as ready as you can. I am already making arrangements for our first mission."

"Oh, really?" I asked. "Where are we going?"

The big Russian thumped the table and took a sip of his wine. "New York City. You are going home, Walt."

CHAPTER 15

"Actually, I grew up in San Diego, but I take your meaning. The good ol' USA, huh?"

"Well," Kamenev said with a smirk. "There are two potential cases, and the one in New York is showing the most promise. There is more investigation to be done, but it looks likely."

"I think I'd like to see the sights in the big apple." I looked at Irina. "Would you like that?"

Her eyes were huge. "Oh yes, Walt."

"I know the city," Shaw volunteered. He looked at Sergei and then the rest of the team. "Be happy to take my brothers and sisters in arms on a tour."

Kamenev raised his wine glass to all of us. "A toast, again ... to the Medusa Division."

"The Medusa Division!" we all called back. It was growing on me.

"Please order dessert or a drink and enjoy each other's company," our Russian host encouraged. "Not too much, though. Our two youngsters have to train tomorrow,"

Irina shook a fist at her father, and we all had a good laugh. The rest of the night was magical. The wine flowed, and people moved seats to talk about their end of the bargain and the mission that might be coming our way. Shaw, Sergei, and Oleg sat together and were talking about guns and other tactical needs. Warmed my heart to see these warriors from opposite sides of the world talking to each other ... and enjoying it.

The three women came together at the end of the table, looking lovely and chatting away. Harada sat close, watching over Kimiko. Irina surprised me, but she was talking to both Darya and Kimiko, switching between Russian and English. They were getting loud, and the wine was definitely having an effect.

That left Kamenev and I sitting beside each other. I ordered a coffee from the waiter and looked at our host. "Thanks for this, Comrade. Such a great gesture, and I can tell everyone is loving this."

"You are welcome. It is a good start."

I sipped my coffee and looked at the group as I spoke to him. "How likely is this mission in New York?"

Kamenev lowered his voice so only I could hear. "It is assured. I only have to finalize the particulars and payment."

"Ah, we're doing this for money?"

"*Da*," he laughed. "Bullets and fancy dinners cost money, Walt."

I laughed, too, and held up my coffee cup. He tapped it with his wine glass, and we laughed anew after a sip of our drink.

****

It was two weeks of hard work. Lots of weights, specifically compound movements, to get our strength up, and a ton of weapons training. We had just finished our final workout. Sergei called us into the center of the dark basement Irina and I had come to call "the dungeon." He put his hands on his hips and looked at Darya. "What are our final numbers?"

The woman looked at a clipboard. "Irina has excelled in everything. She can lift world records in weights, and she was able to jump to a height of seven feet. She is incredibly accurate with a crossbow, and Oleg has trained her to use two gladius swords in close combat. With her strength and speed, nobody can match her."

I looked at Irina and we both smiled. A far cry from the lost young woman I met at the facility in Japan. She had found her purpose and her place in the world. I was *so happy* for her.

"And Walt?" Sergei asked.

Darya turned the page. She looked at me and

reported. "His bench press has gone from a low start to confidence with two-hundred pounds. He can deadlift three hundred pounds, and Oleg is impressed with the way he uses a shield and mace." She set down the clipboard and looked right at me as she spoke. "He has improved a great deal in very little time. Most satisfactory."

Sergei nodded and looked at the ground as he spoke. "This is it. That was our last workout. It is time to say our goodbyes."

It was shocking. We were used to a routine, and each other's company, and it was over. I walked over to Oleg and held out my hand. The big goon grabbed my wrist and pulled me into a bear hug. "*Udachi*, Walt," I heard him mumble.

We broke apart, and I actually saw a mist in the old guy's eyes. "Thanks, Oleg. I'll need it."

Darya and Irina were embracing, and both teared up as they chatted away in Russian. I didn't understand it all, but it was clear that Irina and Darya had forged a friendship. It was touching. Russians have big hearts, but they don't give them easily.

When they came apart, Darya turned her attention to me. The tears were still there as she placed her hands against my cheek. "*Syn Meduzy*," she whispered and kissed me on both cheeks. She looked over her shoulder at Irina and then turned to me. "Take care of each other, okay?"

I smiled and nodded. "Thank you for everything, Darya."

Sergei shook hands with his two friends and turned to us, holding up a phone. "Comrade Kamenev has informed me that you are to pack a bag tonight. A car will meet you at seven in the morning to take you to the airport. The entire team is flying to America. New York city!"

CHAPTER 16

Irina and I woke and grabbed the bags we packed the night before. We traveled light, figuring we could purchase whatever we needed when we got to our destination. We each had a shoulder bag, as well as the black case that contained my unique mace. The second we stepped into the cold Moscow air, a black car pulled in, and a driver hopped out. He was wearing a Russian military uniform, making it clear that this was the ride that Kamenev promised.

He gave us a wave and took our luggage to the trunk. Irina greeted him, and he said something about the weather. My Russian wasn't great, but I could get the gist of their polite conversation.

We drove to the Sheremetyevo International Airport, but we didn't stop where people were being dropped off. Our driver blew by the tourists and businessmen and found a gate manned by a couple of soldiers with rifles. He slowed as they held up a hand, wound down the window, and the briefest of conversations. I was sure I heard the word "Kamenev" in their exchange. I made up my mind that one day, I was going to find out who Irina's father really was and what he did.

The car moved past the workers and planes of every size, and a familiar-looking Learjet came into view. It was the very same plane that took me to Japan when all this madness began. I guessed that Oyabun was providing the transportation. Despite the animosity the two countries had for each other, he and Kamenev had a mutual respect and always seemed to find a way to do business. Lucky for us.

Our driver handed us our bags and gave us a quick salute as we marched toward the stairs toward the open doors. We climbed the stairs quickly and were happy to step into the warm environment of the sleek jet.

Shaw was waiting for us, wearing a coat over his military uniform. "Glad you made it. Now I can close this door," he said with a chuckle. "Moscow's winter is no joke."

Kamenev was just behind him. "You are mistaken, Comrade Shaw. This is a Russian summer. Winter is much colder."

The four of us laughed, and Irina's father took our bags and gestured with his head to move to the passenger area. "When you are seated, we will take off, and the mission briefing will begin."

We put our bags in the overhead bins and greeted the rest of the team. They were all there. Sergei, Harada, Kimiko, and Shaw. The Green Beret took his seat right after we put on our seatbelts.

The jet taxied into position and immediately blasted down the runway and into the air. The short wait made me wonder if we jumped the line at the airport. It seemed likely.

When we achieved altitude, and the seatbelt sign came off, Kamenev stood up and buttoned his suit jacket. "We left a little early. A good start." He looked at every face and smiled. "This is a team that can accomplish anything, and we are answering our first call." He nodded toward Shaw, who was seated beside the dark-bearded Sergei.

He cleared his throat and spoke up. "Our equipment is on the way to Kennedy International Airport in a military transport provided by our Russian friends. Sergei and I were able to make some decisions on weaponry and ammunition."

Kamenev held up a hand to stop him. "What did you decide, if you don't mind telling us."

Shaw looked at Sergei and they both smiled. "It was a compromise. After spending time on the range, we decided on two weapons. American and Russian."

"I was quite impressed with the AR-15 rifle.

Accurate, light, and reliable after modification." Sergei explained.

Shaw nodded. "We opted for a shorter barrel modification in case the vampires get, well, grabby."

"*Da*," Sergei agreed. "For the pistol, we have decided on the Russian Spetsnaz favorite. We will be using the GSh-18, 9mm."

"It's a nice gun," Shaw said with a nod. He looked at Kimiko. "The doctor and our allies in Japan were able to help us with ammunition."

The doctor gave a wan smile. "Yes. We found that polymer bullets were effective in the pistols, but we had to use hollow-point bullets for the rifles as the muzzle velocity is so much faster."

I raised my hand. "Uh, not a gun guy, but wouldn't hollow points work against anyone who was not a vampire?"

"That is an unintentional benefit," the doctor agreed. She looked at everyone in the plane. "The hollow points have been filled with Walt's DNA, and secured with some glue, and capped with a small piece of bamboo. They have proven to be exceptional in testing."

Shaw smiled. "The three of us, Sergei, Harada, and I, will be wearing tactical vests that hold ten magazines, which are roughly three-hundred rounds each. I will also carry a one-shot M72 rocket launcher."

Everyone's eyes widened. I was the one to ask the obvious question. "Shaw, why in God's name would you want a rocket launcher?"

He and Sergei looked at each other and laughed. "I've only used it a couple of times, but I've got to tell you, I'd rather have it and not use it than the other way around." He looked over at Harada. "You won't mind me having one of those, will you friend?"

Harada smiled slowly. "Sound good," he said with a thick Japanese accent. We all laughed at his thinly veiled enthusiasm.

Kamenev held a hand to get everyone's attention. "Walt, you and Irina will have equipment waiting for you when we arrive. A pair of Gladius styled swords to go with Irina's tactical crossbow and bolts." A smile crept on his face. "I have also included a shield to match your mace and a titanium breastplate to protect you both."

I nodded at the man in charge. "*Spasibo*, Comrade. Can you tell us more about our first mission?"

Kamenev nodded. "*Da*, it is to investigate a very old hotel in New York. A fantastic architectural marvel that has seen a few odd and inexplicable homicides."

I looked at Irina and back at her father. "What is the hotel called, if you don't mind me asking."

The Russian shrugged, "It is called 'The Beekman Hotel,' and it is in the heart of the financial district. A wonderful hotel, I am told."

"Does anyone have a laptop? Can we check with the pilots to see if we can use the internet? I'd like to learn more about this place before we touch down."

Harada raised a hand and pulled out a thin, silver laptop. "Try this."

Kamenev walked up to the cockpit and came back a moment later. "This aircraft is equipped with Wi-Fi, and you are welcome to use it."

"Thanks," I said as I took the computer and fired it up. A moment later, I was looking at pictures of a magnificent hotel that was luxurious and old. "It says here that the place was built in 1881. That is one old hotel."

"*Da*," Kamenev agreed. "They are desperate to solve this puzzle. We are being well-paid to remove this issue from this beautiful and historic place. The manager will explain in more detail when we get there."

I grinned. "You think they would be open to letting us stay there a few days, you know ... to investigate?"

Everyone on the plane smiled at the idea, and Kamenev winked at me. "Perhaps something could be worked out."

CHAPTER 17

We touched down at Kennedy International Airport, and Kamenev addressed us all. "Walt and Irina will accompany me to a meeting with the manager of the Beekman Hotel. You are to check your equipment in the hangar that houses our military transport plane and be ready to move in a few hours. I recommend getting lunch at the airport, and I will make arrangements for your accommodation."

Everyone started grabbing their bags, but Kamenev put a hand on my arm to stop me. "We will come back for your luggage. Right now, you and Irina need to come with me."

A limousine rolled onto the tarmac, and we walked through the cold winter air into the long, black car. It was warm inside. The driver must have known the destination because, without a word, we started rolling down the road.

Kamenev undid the buttons on his coat and sat back into the comfortable seat. "I am hoping we did not come all this way for nothing. All indications are that this old hotel is experiencing some kind of vampire activity, but nothing is for certain."

Irina was holding my hand and looking out the window. She was listening but taking in the sights as well. I undid my own coat and looked at her father. "What are we trying to accomplish at this meeting?"

"A few things," he answered with a shrug. "If vampires are indeed causing the strange events at the hotel, and to convince the owner that he needs to allow us to fulfill our purpose, for a price."

I looked out the same window Irina was staring out. "Well, the first part is easy enough. Between the evidence and Irina's enhanced senses, we'll know if anyone infected with the virus is nearby."

"You think the second part will be harder?" he asked.

"Well, it's hard to convince someone you are an expert in something where there are no experts."

Kamenev raised his eyebrows and gestured with his head toward Irina. "You think there is anyone on earth with more experience than you two?"

****

We rolled through the financial district in New York City. Irina's eyes darted left and right, staring through the tinted windows at the skyscrapers and the locals. "So many people doing so many things," she whispered.

I smiled. "It's said that this is the town that never sleeps."

"Looking at all this activity, I believe it," Kamenev mused.

The car rolled down Beekman Street, so I knew we were getting close. I was surprised when we turned onto Nassau Street, and the car came to a halt in front of a relatively small entrance. There on the awning were the words, "The Beekman." We had arrived.

An old-fashioned doorman in a red coat and matching hat opened our door with white-gloved hands and welcomed us. Kamenev got out first and nodded his appreciation. Irina followed her father, and I was the last out. I thanked the doorman, and he smiled politely, but I also noted a look of suspicion. It made me wonder how much the people who worked at the hotel really knew.

The tiles on the floor were small, and a mosaic that formed an intricate design of white tile with black lines that formed a unique, hexagonal design. The walls had square moldings made of dark wood, and old photographs and paintings hung tastefully. There were antique rugs draped over a brass bar on the reception desk and four antique lamps that gave off a gentle glow. The long desk was illuminated by natural light that came from above. It was breathtaking.

Irina grabbed my arm tight as we walked. I looked down at her, and there was no mistaking that look on her face. I'd seen it before. There were vampires around, and she could smell them.

We were received at the front desk by an older woman with a pleasant and professional smile. "Welcome to the Beekman. What can we do for you today?"

The big Russian stepped closer. "Good day. My name is Ivan Kamenev, and we are expected by a mister Martin Scott."

She smiled a little wider and grabbed a phone. She whispered something into the phone, and a moment later, two men in grey suits walked into the lobby and greeted us. The taller one had greasy, receding dark hair and an odd smirk on his face as he held out his hand to us. "Hello, I'm Martin Scott, the manager of the Beekman. This gentleman is Agent Boland of the FBI."

The smaller man had alert, intelligent eyes and a square jaw. He had the face of a fighter, and his eyes were always moving. He didn't miss anything.

"I am Ivan Kamenev," the big Russian said, gesturing toward us. "This is Walt Baranov and my daughter, Irina."

Everyone shook hands, but I detected an air of suspicion from the manager of the hotel. He leaned closer to Kamenev and said, "We should have this conversation in private. In my office, if you please."

We followed the man to a spacious office with two nice chairs in front of the vast, black desk. There were two other chairs in the corners of the office. There was a picture of his wife, and a nameplate said, "M. Scott" on his desk. Funny, I remembered Ivan had a nameplate on his desk when we first met, but it was plain brass and stated his name as a simple fact. This black nameplate with the fancy gold script and edges seemed pretentious. The guy thought a lot of himself.

Kamenev and I sat in front of the big desk while Irina sat behind us in one corner, and Boland took the other chair. The Russian sat down with a sigh and looked at the man behind the desk. "Mister Martin Scott, why are we here today? Why have you called us?"

The manager shrugged, and an odd smile came to his lips. It was arrogance personified. "I'm not sure why either. You came highly recommended by some of the higher-ups in the FBI. We have a few missing person issues that remain unsolved. Our evidence is not adding up and your name was mentioned as the one to solve it. Why is that?"

"We have experience with … the unusual," Kamenev replied.

"What is it you do, exactly?" Scott asked with

disdain.

"As I said, we have experience with the unusual, and we help others with less experience."

The manager raised an eyebrow. "I don't understand that explanation."

Kamenev smiled, "Perhaps it would be best if you shared your problems with us. Then we can tell you what we have to offer."

Scott looked at officer Boland and sighed. "Very well. There have been a few disappearances that we have not been able to explain or solve."

"How many?" I asked.

He looked down at the desk. "Over the last six months, there have been eleven."

"We think it might be more," Boland explained. "This is only what we know as of right now."

"Guests or employees?" Kamenev asked.

"Both," Scott mumbled. "At first, it was the kitchen and cleaning staff. We thought it was just a matter of employee absenteeism. Then, relatives of guests who didn't check out started calling after loved ones who had disappeared. Their luggage still sat in their rooms."

"A serial killer?" I asked.

Boland shook his head. "That was our first thought, then things got weird."

"How?" Kamenev asked.

The manager started tapping his desk with a finger. "Two of the missing young women were seen and positively identified by guests. When spotted, they turned and ran. They just disappeared."

"They just ran away? That is weird." I agreed.

"Yes, they vanished again. No trace." The manager looked up from his desk into Kamenev's eyes. "But that is not the reason we called you."

The Russian gestured with his hand. "Please, continue."

Scott sat forward in his seat and put his elbows on the table. "A guest was attacked in our hotel outside his room. The assailant fled when other guests happened upon the crime. The victim was badly injured, particularly in the neck area. He was treated for some kind of odd infection."

I heard Irina draw a sharp breath behind me and pretended I didn't. "Did the guest survive?"

Scott shrugged, "Yes, the victim made a full recovery, but it's the next piece of evidence that really threw us."

The manager looked at Boland, and something unsaid passed between them. He stood up from his desk, retrieved an old black and white picture from a shelf, and handed it to Kamenev. "You see the man in the very front at the far left?"

"Yes," the Russian answered and handed the

picture to me. I saw a tall man with dark hair, greasy and parted on the side.

"The witnesses saw that picture hanging in the bar and were adamant that he was the attacker. The victim identified the man in that picture in the hospital. His name is Claude Borges."

I frowned at the manager. "Did you arrest the man?"

He shook his head. "Look at the date in the picture. Borges was a lawyer here in 1883 before it was a hotel. About one hundred and forty years ago."

The silence hung in the air. I looked at Kamenev, who looked over his shoulder at his daughter. Irina gave a slight, slow nod.

Kamenev turned to the man behind the desk. "Your problem is easy to identify. You have a vampire in your hotel. Probably more than one."

CHAPTER 18

The silence hung in the air until the manager snorted and sat back in his chair, putting his hands on his belly. "Really? You must be joking."

"Not at all," Kamenev said. "It is an explanation that addresses all of the mysteries and inconsistencies in your story."

Scott shook his head, and that smug, sardonic smile appeared on his face. "Agent Boland, I do believe we have some con artists in the room. Have you heard enough to arrest them?"

Boland shrugged and spread his hands apart. "If you remember, I was the one who went to my department seeking additional expertise. Comrade Kamenev comes highly recommended."

Kamenev turned to look at the officer and gave him a smile. "What was it that convinced you that something unique was happening here?"

The agent rubbed his neck and shook his head, looking at the floor. "When the witnesses identified

Claude Borges, I thought they were drunk or just plain wrong." He let out a sigh and smiled. "Until I saw some security footage, and I'm telling you, it's him. Not a double. It is absolutely him."

The manager of the hotel sneered at him. "Couldn't you be mistaken as well?"

"Sure," Boland laughed. "So I ran stills from the security footage against the picture with face-recognition software. It was a perfect match."

Scott still wore the stupid smirk, but his eyes told a different story. "What happens now? What would you do to solve this issue?"

Kamenev smiled and gestured with a hand towards me. "I would like my two experts to explore your hotel and see what they can discover."

"And what would that cost?" the manager asked with a frown.

"Nothing for an evaluation. However, if they discover any evidence of vampire activity, you know the terms of service, and the contract was emailed to you two days ago."

Scott stood up and paced behind his desk, rubbing his chin. He looked at me, then Irina. He gave a prissy little snort. "These are your 'vampire experts?' What are you trying to pull, Kamenev?"

The unflappable Russian gave a slow shrug. "You simply will not find two people with more experience in these matters. Mister Baranov has personally dispatched countless numbers of these monsters, and my daughter has heightened senses that allow her to detect them, among other talents."

The manager sat back down in his chair, and his mouth twisted into a crooked smile. "I'm looking at a young man barely out of his teens, you dub a vampire killer and a little girl who has 'heightened senses?' What does that even mean?"

Irina stood up and walked to the middle of the office. I didn't like the look on her face. She took a deep breath in through her nose and closed her eyes. She glared at the manager. "You are a coffee drinker, and you had some kind of meat with a lot of onions for lunch."

Scott's eyes were a little larger, but he still had that stupid smile. "I did have a hot dog extra onions, but this is just a third-rate magic trick—"

"You also have two strong scents on your person." Irina interrupted with a smirk of her own. "I smell your cologne, and you also smell of the same perfume that the woman at the front desk was wearing. I wonder why that is?"

The manager stopped smiling, his face turned red, and his mouth hung open. "How dare you!"

"Look," Boland stood up and spoke. "They come with a full-recommendation from the FBI, and there's no charge for them to look around. What's the harm in that?"

Kamenev stood, too. "If we don't find anything that convinces you we are correct, you can always refuse. You have the final say."

It was funny to watch the man's face turn from red to white as he composed himself. "Very well, I will allow you to investigate the hotel, but you are not allowed to speak a word of this to the guests nor the hotel employees. Understood?"

"No problem," I said with a smile. "If there's anything to find, we'll find it."

I got up to stand beside Kamenev. The Russian offered the manager his hand and wore a gentle smile. "Goodbye for now. We will talk again, Comrade Scott."

The manager nodded, looking at the floor. "Agent Boland, could you remain? I'd like a private word with you."

Boland smiled and moved to one of the chairs and sat down while the three of us made our way to the door.

Kamenev opened the door for his daughter, but she stopped before crossing the threshold and looked back at the two men in the office. "Agent Boland, you may want to talk to Mister Scott about the drugs he is keeping in the top drawer of his desk."

She walked out without another word, and we

followed her, closing the door on the conversation the smug manager didn't want. I wish I could have been a fly on the wall for that little talk.

CHAPTER 19

"Irina," Kamenev growled to his daughter as we walked back to the lobby. "That was not prudent."

She didn't look at him as she scowled. "I didn't like that man. He is pig."

"He is *a* pig," I corrected.

She grinned at me. "He is *A DIRTY* pig!"

Kamenev couldn't help a small smile as we entered the beautiful lobby. "After we get the money, you can say whatever you want to him, daughter. That is just good business."

I looked up into the natural light and saw floor after floor above us. "What do you think about starting at the top floor and working our way down?"

"*Da*, that makes sense." Kamenev agreed.

We made our way to an old elevator that reminded me of the one in Kamenev's building in Russia. I hated these things. It was in better shape, and it was a smoother, quieter ride. "Do you smell anything, Irina?" I asked.

She shook her head. "There is a scent of vampires in this hotel, but there is nothing in the elevator."

The elevator stopped at the top floor, and we stepped out into the hallway. I walked to the edge of the rail and looked down, deep into the center of the lobby. "Wow! That is a long way down."

"This way," Kamenev called, and he led the way. Irina took my arm as we walked.

"I smell them," she whispered to us after an old couple passed us. "It is strong on this floor."

"See, that's weird. They were on the top floor but didn't use the elevator? Irina, vampires can't fly, can they?"

"*Nyet*, Walt. It is curious." She stopped when she came to a wall. "Here. A strong smell of blood and vampires right here."

Kamenev and I looked at each other. "It is a wall, daughter. Nothing more."

I looked closer at the square wooden molding. I moved to the wall and ran my hand over the surface until I found a couple of deep scratches. "What is this?" I wondered aloud.

Irina gently put her hands on my shoulders and steered me away. She was still breathing deep through her nose, and her eyes narrowed as she looked at the scratches. She suddenly hit the wall with both hands, and a panel slid up, revealing a large, rectangular hole in the wall.

"Whoa!" I laughed, and all three of us got closer to the hole and peered into the darkness. We saw spider webs, a brick wall, and ropes that dangled in the middle of the void. I stuck my head in and looked down into the darkness. It looked like it went all the way to the floor. "It's a dumb waiter," I said.

The two Russians frowned at me. "What is 'dumb waiter?' I do not understand," Irina asked.

I leaned back, away from the hole in the wall. "A dumb waiter is a box that's like a little elevator. The kitchen or bar could put supplies in the box and use the ropes to move it up to other floors. But this place was originally a law office. Maybe they used it to move big, heavy files? It would be a lot easier than carrying them up the stairs or to the elevator. The shaft is larger than you would expect. It was an interesting idea but a very old one."

Kamenev shrugged. "This is a very old hotel. This would explain how these creatures are appearing and disappearing."

Irina hit the panel again and it fell back into place neatly. Unless you knew it was there, it was doubtful anyone would detect it. She looked at me and nodded her agreement.

I rubbed my chin and stared at the wall. "I don't think they had doors like that in the past. I'm thinking someone altered it to make it easy to open and close. They would have to know the hotel pretty well. I mean, who would even know the old dumb waiter is there?"

"A lawyer that was here from the start, like Claude Borges," Kamenev answered. "He would know."

Irina started walking. "Come, I smell something else on this floor. Something that should not be here."

Kamenev gave me a wary look and gestured for me to go first. I knew how he felt. Irina was concentrating, and her face grew harder. The way it always did when vampires were nearby.

Irina was walking at a pretty good clip and then stopped dead in the hallway. She slowly turned and pointed at a door with the number 912 on the door. "This room. It smells of vampires and blood." She looked at me with cold eyes. "There is death in that room."

CHAPTER 20

Kamenev used his phone to call the front desk and let them know we needed access to a room. A minute later, a small man in a grey three-piece suit and round glasses came speed-walking down the hall. "Hello there. I'm Steven Brown. I'm the assistant manager at the hotel." He had a key in his hand and used his other hand to push his dark hair back off his face. He stopped and took a moment to catch his breath. "Whew! I got here as fast as I could."

"*Spasibo*, Comrade Brown," Kamenev said with a smile. "Would you please grant us access to room 912? We have reason to believe there is something amiss."

"Very well," he agreed and knocked on the door loudly. "Hello! Management here. Is there anybody inside?" He looked at us. "Sorry, that's protocol."

"Nobody will answer you," Irina said softly.

He looked at her and frowned. "Oh, that's worrisome." He let out a sigh and used his key.

"Coming in!" he announced to anyone who might hear. Nobody would answer him, and it became apparent the moment we crossed the threshold.

It was a stench that hit you the second you walked in. Rot, decay, and a few flies were buzzing around the place. We could see some blood on the small area rug at the foot of the bed. A small, bare foot was also visible, and it was white, with a purplish bruise formed at the heel.

"Oh, my God!" Brown said, putting his hand over his mouth and nose.

Irina walked to the bed as cool as you please and looked at the body in the bed. Kamenev and I were just behind her. It was an older woman in white flannel pajamas that were stained with blood. Grey hair was splayed across the bloody pillow. Her wide eyes stared at the ceiling, and the wound on her neck was obvious.

"Should I call the police?" Brown asked Kamenev.

"*Nyet*, you should go downstairs and alert Agent Boland and the manager. They have a murder to investigate, and this poor woman's body must be prepared for removal and burial."

I really liked the old Russian. He was tough, shrewd, but the guy had a heart. I liked him long before I fell in love with this daughter. I know it's weird, but looking at the poor old lady who lost everything and then considering what I'd been through, I felt lucky. Very lucky.

"You're right. Are you staying here?" Brown asked as he turned to leave.

"*Da*, we will stay with her and look around the room for anything that might reveal the killer."

"Okay, but don't touch anything," the small man instructed before he jogged out of the room.

I looked at Irina. "Vampire, no doubt. Right?"

She shook her head. "This is bad. This vampire killed woman and did not dispose of body. That is against rules."

"And no effort was made to disguise the neck wound," Kamenev observed with a frown.

"That's offside in the vampire world, isn't it?" I asked Irina.

"*Da*, this is a vampire who does not know better," she explained.

"A new one?"

She looked at me and then her father. "*Da*. A new one."

Agent Boland, Martin Scott, and the assistant manager came to the door together. Boland walked in first and his alert eyes found the body and looked all around the room. "No forced entry, and the cause of death looks obvious. Nothing conclusive until we hear from the coroner, but it does match something we've seen before in this hotel."

Martin Scott sneered, but his eyes were defeated as he looked at Kamenev. "Okay, what do you want to solve this?"

The Russian smiled. "You know our fee, but we will also need skeleton keys for the hotel. I will be bringing in four more members of my team to deal with this. We will find the vampire responsible for this, and it will be dealt with. You have my word."

The manager held up a finger. "Okay, fine. But this must be kept quiet. I do not want your team trampling through the hotel like Nazi stormtroopers and terrifying our guests. Is that understood?"

Kamenev nodded. "That is agreeable."

I held up a hand to my face as if I were bothered by the smell and whispered, knowing only one person would be able to hear me.

Irina turned to the manager. "After we kill vampires, we need to stay here for three full days. They are very territorial, and we need to make sure that none remain."

His mouth turned into that weird, smug smile. "Oh really? And you're the vampire expert, right?"

Whoops!

Irina walked right up to him, eyes cold, looking up at the taller man. "Yes, I am an expert on vampires. Do you want to know why?"

He rolled his eyes and shrugged. "Okay."

She glared at him and her voice was like ice. "*I used to be one.*" Without another word, she turned away from the stunned man and left the room.

You had to love her.

CHAPTER 21

"Wait, did you say we've got three free days at a luxury hotel in New York city?" Shaw asked. The entire team was meeting in a hangar at the airport, and we were bringing them up to speed.

"It is true," Kamenev said. "I am as surprised as you are."

"Well, I may have whispered a suggestion to Irina," I said with a grin. She looked at me and started to giggle.

"What did she say?" Sergei asked with a frown.

Irina shrugged, "I told them we would have to remain for three days because vampires are territorial. We must ensure they do not return."

Doctor Kimiko shook her head and pointed at us. "That's not true, is it?"

"Of course not," I answered.

The team looked at each other and started laughing. "Well, alright!" Shaw cheered.

"It gets better," I interrupted. "You guys are

welcome to eat at the hotel restaurant, drink at the hotel bar, and I'll pick up the tab. This one's on me, guys."

There were cheers again, and a few of them shook my hand or gave me a pat on the back. Sergei gave me a quick salute, and Harada bowed low, which I returned.

"But there are vampires in the hotel? We know this for sure?" Kimiko asked.

"Oh yes," Kamenev answered. "We found one of their victims. An unfortunate woman who was killed in her room."

"That's kind of sloppy for these guys, isn't it?" Shaw asked.

"Yes," Kimiko replied. "It is not acceptable in the vampire community. They are always to dispose of the body or cover their tracks by making it look like anything other than a vampire attack."

"We think it is a new vampire. One who doesn't know any better who killed the woman. But, there's more to this story." I took a breath and looked at each of them. They were all focused. "There have been sightings of a guy called Claude Borges who used to work at the place before it was a hotel. He worked there in 1883. We think he's an old vampire who is creeping around the hotel."

"Interesting. What's the plan?" Shaw asked.

Kamenev held up a hand. "Everyone gets a room. You are to appear as guests of the hotel, nothing more."

"Tourists?" Sergei guessed.

"Yes, exactly," I answered. "And be careful what you say. You never know who is listening," I said with a wink at Irina.

"Have your equipment ready so you can mobilize with a moment's notice," Kamenev instructed us. "You may have a few days in a beautiful hotel, but there is still work to be done."

"The equipment," Sergei announced. "We should try our best to make sure everything fits and everything is here."

"Suit up!" Shaw called to all of us.

****

Fifteen minutes later, we were wearing our uniforms, and our gear was strapped on. It was quite the assortment of warriors.

Sergei and Shaw wore black tactical vests over dark olive fatigues that were jammed full of magazines; their black combat boots shined. A pistol was holstered on their hip, and the short-barreled AR-15 rifles were expertly strapped to their shoulders. They also had the small M72 rocket launchers on a strap. Their helmets had night vision goggles attached, and they wore amber sharpshooting glasses. In the center of their tactical vests was a white graphic of Medusa's face.

Harada wore the same olive fatigues but only pistols. No rifle and no helmet. There was one on his hip, another in a shoulder holster, and I watched him strap a small gun into a devious ankle holster. The Medusa symbol was etched into the leather of the holsters and on the handles of the guns. Those were the Yakuza gangster's weapons of war.

Kimiko wore a long, black coat that was similar to her lab coat, but it had many more pockets to hold her equipment. She wore black boots that went to her knee, jeans, and a turtleneck. Her glasses looked more like safety goggles, and she was checking the tools in her black doctor's bag.

I laughed when I saw what Kamenev had selected for me. An olive shirt without arms was to be worn beneath a metal breastplate that had been painted green. It was quite light and fit well. It felt comfortable and allowed my arms a great range of motion.

I found a helmet that looked like something from ancient Rome. It was something you would expect a centurion to wear. It covered my whole head but had holes for my eyes to see and a bar that came down to protect my nose.

Kamenev walked toward me with something under his arm. "To go with your mace," he said as he handed me a shield. And what a shield! Large, round, light, and Medusa's face took up the whole thing. The mythical gorgon's eyes and fangs snarled at the world while the snakes that made up her hair framed the fearsome visage.

"Wow! Thank you so much, Mister Kamenev, but isn't it a little much?"

"Wait until you see my little girl," he said with a grin.

I looked at Irina. He wasn't exaggerating. Without a doubt, she was the most impressive member of the group. She had an olive breastplate like me, with a white Medusa graphic on the chest, but that was all we had in common.

Irina wore high, black boots that buckled closed all the way to her knee. Black leather pants protected her upper legs, and a quiver of bolts dangled at her hip. The tactical crossbow was in her hands, and she was checking it. Handles from two gladius-styled swords peeked over her shoulders. They were strapped to her back, so she just had to reach back to draw them in a hurry.

The most impressive part of her uniform was the helmet. It was like my gladiator-styled model, but where mine was plain on top, hers had this large plume of black horse hair that stuck straight up, and longer strands at the back of the helmet fell down her back. It made her look taller and fierce.

Kamenev clapped his hands together three times to get our attention. "This ... this is exactly what I envisioned. A team that would inspire fear in these creatures." He looked at me. "One of their most feared legends come to life, and a team behind him. You are ready."

I took off my helmet and pointed my mace at Irina. "I know they'll be scared of me, but I think she's going to command their attention too."

The Russian laughed. "They will be frightened of you, Walt. They all know the legend. They will learn to fear Irina. She is their nemesis."

CHAPTER 22

After changing back into our street clothes, we packed our gear into black bags. I walked by Kimiko and whispered in her ear. She looked up at me with wide eyes, and a smile grew on her face. "Not a bad idea, Walt."

A small fleet of cabs arrived at the hangar to take us to the hotel. They were all from different companies. It was a brilliant cover. Nobody, seeing any of us arrive, would ever suspect we were all one big happy team of vampire slayers.

Harada wore an expensive and elegant grey suit, and he was posing as a Japanese businessman. He would play the part well.

Sergei and Shaw were sharing a cab and rooming close to each other. They were pretending to be soldiers on leave, whooping it up in the Big Apple. They genuinely liked each other and were sure to be convincing.

Kamenev and Kimiko had their own cabs, and

their own rooms. He was supposed to be a Russian investor, in town for a few meetings. She was to be a Japanese banker here to meet with the manager of a large investment firm.

Irina and I had the easiest role of all. We were playing the young couple in love, enjoying a trip to New York City. Which was perfect because we were in love and certainly planning on having fun after subduing some troublesome vampires.

Everyone knew their role, and Kamenev let us know that the assistant manager, Steven Brown, would carefully leak these cover stories to the staff in the hotel. This would allow us to hunt and encourage the vampires to hunt us. My hands began to sweat just thinking about it.

Our cab pulled up to the Beekman, and we got out. The doorman greeted us as we entered the hotel, and we held hands as we walked through the majestic lobby. The natural light that came down from the large skylight above guided us to the dark hardwood desk and Turkish rugs of the reception area.

A young woman with the darkest skin, wearing a crisp white shirt with a blue vest, smiled at us as we approached. I saw a nametag that read "Candace." She gave us a million-dollar smile, and her musical voice greeted us. "Welcome to the Beekman Hotel. How may I help you?"

"Hi, I have a reservation. My last name is Baranov."

She looked at her computer screen and smiled again. "Yes, Mister Baranov. I have your reservation here. I see you are checking in today ... but there is no checkout date?"

I looked down into the lovely dark eyes of the young woman on my arm. I got lost for a moment.

"Mister Baranov? Your checkout date?"

"Oh, sorry. Well ... we haven't decided on that. Not sure how long it will take us to see everything there is to see. Can we leave it open?"

She nodded. "Yes, but I'll need a larger deposit. Is that okay?"

I looked at Irina and smiled, then turned back. "Sure!"

We took care of the financial arrangements, and Candace handed me our key. "Enjoy your stay at the Beekman."

I looked down again at Irina and she smiled up at me. I didn't look at the friendly employee when I answered. I was too busy admiring the young woman beside me. "Thanks so much. I'm sure our stay will be memorable."

We grabbed our bags, filled with armor and weaponry, and started walking toward the elevator. Irina started giggling and leaned into me as we were walking.

"What's got you laughing?" I asked.

"The girl who helped us. After we leave, she say to girl beside her, 'One day, I want to find a man who looks at me the way he looks at her.'"

CHAPTER 23

We held hands as we crossed the spacious atrium of the hotel, past a large and comfortable sofa, and to the Augustine restaurant. We waited to be seated and took in the place as we made our way to the table.

The first thing that caught my eye was the bar and the bottles behind it. The shelves of drinks went up to the roof, and it was backlit, so the bottles glowed. The dark, hardwood bar was topped in marble, and the brass rail was very old-school. You'd think you had stepped back in time a hundred years if not for the glow of the computer screens where the servers tallied their bills. Shaw and Sergei were sitting down and having a drink. They didn't look up or acknowledge us in any way. Good! Just a couple of young men drinking in New York, and nobody would think otherwise.

Our hostess walked us into the restaurant and to our seats. Large orb lights hung from the ceiling and gave off a dull glow. It lit the place up enough that you could see what you were doing, but it was also subdued and relaxed. All the seats had white tablecloths and cloth napkins folded to sit high on their plates. Every table was for four people, and there was a couple that had a long booth-like seat that stretched down one wall. We got one of the ones with the bench seat, and Irina was eager to sit there. I had to remember that as old as she really was, there were so many things that were new to her. I was about to get a painful reminder.

I sat down in one of the dark wood chairs and picked up my leather-backed menu. This was the kind of place Al Capone would have frequented, except this place specialized in French cuisine, not Italian. I looked to my right and saw Harada seated in one corner. Eating by himself and looking at a newspaper from Tokyo. There was no doubt he was reading the room more than he was reading the paper.

If Harada was here, so was Kimiko. Sure enough, a couple of tables away, Kimiko sat eating, but she wasn't alone. A tall, pale redhead with short hair was sitting across from her. Turquoise earrings and a long matching dress worked well with her slender form and skin tone. Kimiko wore a black pantsuit and glasses that didn't have frames. I saw her eyes move my way and then right back to her dinner guest.

Irina's eyes perked up, then she quickly looked back at her menu. I heard her father's voice talking in Russian and stole a glance toward the entrance to the restaurant. He was being shown to a table at a window, and he had two other men with him. They were all of an age, wearing suits and speaking Russian. Okay, I was impressed. The man, posing as a Russian investor, was eating dinner with other Russian investors. Again, I found myself wondering who Kamenev really was. I doubted I'd ever know.

We ordered our appetizers and meals, and I saw Irina frowning. I'd learned long ago that she should never keep anything bottled up. It would eat her until it came out in a way that could get people killed. Not good.

"What's on your mind, Irina?" I asked. "You seem preoccupied."

She didn't look at me but down at her plate as she answered. "You whispered something to Kimiko in the hangar I did not understand."

"Oh!" I laughed. "I just suggested that she might know someone who would be interested in staying in such a beautiful hotel. I suggested that hopping on a flight from San Francisco to New York might make for a romantic working vacation."

"*Nyet*, you said her 'partner' would probably enjoy staying with her. I heard you, Walt."

I frowned at her. "I'm not understanding. Why does this bother you?"

She shrugged. "I expected a man to come, not a

woman. Why is it a woman?"

I sat back in my chair, and my eyes narrowed. "Uh, well, that is who Kimiko loves. Her name is Kim Rourke, and they have been dating almost as long as we have."

Her nose wrinkled, and she reached for her water. "That is disgusting," she mumbled before taking a sip.

Wow! I just stared at her. My eyes were wide, and my mouth hung open. I was speechless.

"Did I say something wrong?" she asked with a small voice.

Part of me wanted to say everything was wrong with that, but I had to remember who she was and what she had been through. I was looking at a young woman who was a vampire for decades. She was a very traditional woman with some very old-fashioned views. I mean, I had to fight to get her to let me help in the kitchen.

"Irina, I know you have been … in the dark for a very long time." She looked down at her lap, and I hated myself. "It's not your fault," I continued. "Things have changed, and I think for the better."

"What has changed, Walt?"

"Well, for starters, we believe women are equal to men. Have I ever discouraged you from becoming a soldier, a fighter?"

"No, because I am very good," she said with a big smile. You had to love her.

"Yes!" I laughed. "Yes, you are amazing. Imagine if I had a traditional view and said something like, 'No woman of mine will be a fighter.' I mean, how would you like that?"

She frowned. "That would be stupid."

"Yes, it would. We are who we are. You, my darling, are a tough, fearless beauty, and you have stolen my heart. I cannot help but love you."

Irina reached out and took my hand, her eyes tearing up. "I love you too."

"I would never stop you from pursuing your own life. I want you to be happy, and I want you to be true to yourself. I feel the exact same way about Kimiko."

She still held my hand and moved her thumb over my skin. I could tell she was chewing on the idea.

"I know this is a big change, but now people who are attracted to people who are the same gender can get married, have kids. It's okay now."

Letting go of my hand, she sat back in her chair as our appetizers arrived. "That is big change for me, Walt. Not accepted in Russia."

I thanked our server and started getting ready to eat my appetizer. "Oh, there are places where it is still unacceptable, but most people and most places are fine with it."

"Really?"

"Yes. Here's another way to look at it. Does it affect you in any way who Kimiko loves and dates? Does it affect you and me in any way?"

Her eyes searched her food as she picked up a fork. "No, it does not."

"Right! So why should it bother us? Really, why should we care? Nobody is being harmed."

"This is true," she agreed as she put some food in her mouth.

"Sweet Irina, if you're having trouble accepting this, I get it. I'm just asking you to try to understand that Kimiko is happy, and please don't treat her any differently. One of the reasons you're alive is because of her."

Irina ate a few bites of her appetizer and looked up at me. "I can do that. I want Kimiko to be happy, too."

"Thanks," I said. "I believe it will be easier than you think. Kim is a really cool person. She runs her own clothing store in San Francisco. Kimiko says she's funny, and she makes her laugh."

Irina's eyes opened wide, and she dropped her fork. "Walt, the woman in red," she whispered.

I looked over my shoulder quickly to see a tall, blonde woman in a flashy red dress make her way to the end of the bar and sit down. "Yeah, what? Is she ..?"

"Yes, Walt," she whispered. *She is vampire!*"

CHAPTER 24

I touched her hand to get her attention. "Irina, did she hear you?"

"*Nyet*. There is enough noise in the restaurant. She could not hear."

"Okay, good. This is a huge break," I rubbed my chin and thought aloud. "I can't go near her. If I touch her, it's over."

"I can take her," Irina growled. She wasn't kidding, and I had no doubt she could.

"No, no! We need to question her. Find out what is going on here. Besides, the manager, the one you called a pig ... you remember him, right?"

She grinned and nodded.

"He wanted us to work quietly. I'm pretty sure everyone in this restaurant would remember a small, dark-haired beauty like you beating the stuffing out of a vampire with blonde hair in a red dress."

She laughed, and I joined her. The server came back and delivered our entrees. I asked her for a pen.

She handed one to me and left. I grabbed the round cardboard coaster from under my drink and started scribbling. It was a lot to write, and I needed to make sure it all fit. It had to be clear because we were only going to get one shot at this.

I slid the coaster over to Irina, and she took the time to read the note I had written. I looked at the woman in red to make sure she wasn't looking. She was chatting with the bartender, probably prepping him in case she didn't find any other prey. Always good to have a backup.

Leaning closer to my dinner companion, I whispered, "She can't see you do this, okay?"

Irina stood up and walked over to the bar, standing right beside Shaw. I saw her talk to the bartender, and he laughed and let her take a lemon out of a dish. The petite brunette strolled back to our table with a smile on her face and squeezed some lemon into her glass of water. "It is done," she whispered.

"Good!" I laughed. "Now we can enjoy our meal." I picked up my cutlery and started cutting into my dinner, and I saw Shaw walk over to the attractive blonde in the red dress. She gave him a bright smile and started playing with her hair. The game had begun, but she didn't know that the rules had changed and there were many more players.

Irina and I finished our meal, and I looked up at

the bar. Sergei was gone and Shaw was still chatting up the tall blonde. Things were looking good, so we settled our bill, left a generous tip, and left the restaurant hand in hand.

The second we were in the atrium, we marched to the elevator. I looked at Irina. "We've got about five minutes to get back downstairs. Just grab what you need, and we've got to hurry."

"I only need two things," Irina said with a small smile.

"I just need one."

****

Irina and I stood in the alley between the Beekman Hotel and the next building. We were wearing our coats and staring at a steel door. A moment later, the door burst open, and light from the restaurant flashed in the alley. Two people came laughing into the cold New York night. The blonde hair and red dress flashed in the night, and I heard Shaw laughing as they stopped dead. They probably didn't see us standing there in the darkness.

The woman grabbed Shaw by the shoulders and pushed him back into the wall. He was ready for her and pushed back, keeping her at bay. Her mouth opened wide to show misshapen teeth and a couple of fangs as she pressed forward.

Irina took two steps and grabbed a fistful of

blonde hair with both hands. She turned and swung the blonde by the hair, throwing her through the air. She smacked into a brick wall about fifteen feet away. I heard all the air leave her body.

She stood up, groggy and hissing, but Irina was there with two gladius swords in each hand. She put one on either side of the woman's neck, like a pair of scissors, and drove the blades into the wall, pushing her back. The vampire's eyes glowed green in the dark, and her hands came to the blades, but she couldn't move them. Irina was stronger, and she was caught.

"Okay, we need to talk," I said, walking up behind Irina. Shaw came in beside me.

"*Let me GO!*" the thing hissed.

"I need some information first. What is your name?" I asked.

She just screamed and hissed. Irina moved the blades a little closer, and her glowing eyes bulged. "Stop making noise, or I end you," Irina growled.

"Your name. Your *full* name," I pressed.

"*Marie,*" she gasped with that strange, hollow timbre that vampires had. A trickle of her blood ran down Irina's blade. "*Marie Borges.*"

"Borges!" Shaw exclaimed.

I held up a hand to silence him. "Wife of Claude Borges, I'm guessing?"

She stopped struggling and her eyes bored into

mine. She said nothing.

"I'll take that as a yes." I shrugged. "I'm sorry, Marie. It's over. Claude has had his way for a long time, and I'm sure you've been right beside him. But all that is over now."

"*He will kill you for this!*" she snarled.

I walked closer but was careful that she couldn't reach me. Not for my protection but hers. I held up the mace in my hand and pointed to the inscription. "They have nicknamed me 'Medusa's Son.' Do you know what that means?"

Her glowing eyes narrowed. "*It cannot be. That is a myth.*"

"Lady, I've seen what he can do in Japan. Did you hear what went down there?" Shaw asked with a shake of his head.

"Better to show you," I said. I reached up with one finger and touched the trickle of her blood that had pooled by the hilt of Irina's sword. It immediately started bubbling and dissipated to nothing.

The blonde vampire's eyes bulged, and she tried in vain to free herself from Irina's sharp embrace. "*Let me go!*" she whimpered.

"How many? How many people has Claude turned?" I barked.

She started laughing and crying at the same time. "*Over a hundred,*" she cried. "*They will destroy you!*

You cannot hope to defeat that many."

Over a hundred? I didn't expect that answer. How could we deal with that many, and where were they? How could we even find them?

"Just kill me," the thing hissed, and I saw Irina's hands tighten on the grips of the sword.

"Let her go," I said mildly.

Shaw and Irina's heads snapped to stare at me. "Walt, you're not serious?" Shaw asked.

"Yes, I am. Let her go."

Irina drew the swords back, and the vampire fell to her knees, staring up at me and recoiling against the wall. In a flash, Irina had dropped a sword and took a fistful of blonde hair with one hand. She grunted and flung the blonde from the alley into the street. We saw her hit the sidewalk hard, then scramble to her feet and flee, barefoot and snarling.

Shaw and I looked at her with wide eyes. "What?" she said with a shrug. "You said to let her go, so I got rid of her." She wiped the blades on the red high heels the creature left behind and sheathed them. "She's gone. Let's get out of the cold."

CHAPTER 25

Six pairs of eyes were glaring at me, but Kamenev was the one to finally say it. "You let her go? Why did you do that, Walt?" He was subdued, and there was no emotion in the question. He'd been at the top too long to make snap judgements.

We were all meeting in Kamenev's large and opulent suite. I'd requested the meeting, and Kamenev reached out to every member of the team. Kamenev, Kimiko, and Harada were seated while Shaw and Sergei leaned against a wall. I'd told them how Shaw got the blonde vampire outside and what happened.

"I should have killed her," Irina snarled, looking at the ground.

"And then what?" I asked her.

"We are here to kill vampires!" she exclaimed, and I could tell she was fed up with me. They all were.

"Listen, if we'd killed Marie Borges, then we would have accomplished nothing. We know there's more than one vampire involved, she says a hundred."

"We will have to hunt them down," Kamenev said with a nod.

"That's right," I agreed. "After killing Marie, where would you start? We have no idea where they are. They could be anywhere."

Kamenev got up, put some ice cubes in a glass, and poured himself a drink. "I think I see your point, Walt. What do you think you accomplished by letting her go?"

I smiled. "You said it yourself. They are afraid of 'Medusa's Son.' By showing her who I was and that I was real, she's going to go scurrying back to Claude and the others and let them know I'm here. We don't know what we're dealing with. Now, they don't know what they're dealing with either."

Sergei clucked his tongue and shook his head. "You have surrendered the element of surprise. That's why we were all undercover, correct?"

I nodded and pointed at him. "And that was the smart play at the time. Truth is, they don't know about you, Kimiko, or Harada." I smiled at him. "Don't worry, Comrade. There are still a few more surprises in store for these things."

"A hundred," Kimiko whispered. "How can we hope to defeat that many?"

"We can't," I answered with a shrug. "So I'm going to make sure we don't have to."

"What do you have in mind?" Kamenev asked.

"Look, when Marie tells them about me and what Irina did to her, they're going to be freaked out. They're not going to sit in their hole and wait for us to find them. He's going to want to get confirmation, and when he has it, he will move to eliminate us."

"You are flushing them out," Shaw said with a grin.

I smiled back. "Oh yeah, but even more than that. If this goes the way I want, Claude Borges is in for a shock, and our job is going to get a lot easier."

Kamenev took a drink and swirled the ice cubes in his glass. "We are ready to hear your plan, Walt."

I spent the next fifteen minutes talking about what would come next and how we could handle it. I told them what I was hoping to accomplish and how I wanted things to end. When I finished, I looked around the room, trying to read their faces. Nobody seemed hostile, but nobody seemed convinced either.

"I want to kill them all," Irina whispered.

"I know," I laughed. "And with the firepower our team can deliver, you might just do it." I stood up and stretched. "But me? I'm not willing to start a war I can't win."

Kamenev held up his glass in salute. "Very prudent. What will you do now?"

"Go to bed. What else can I do?"

The members of the team all looked at each other and then back at me. "That's it?" Shaw asked. "You're going to bed?"

"Yeah," I answered with a shrug. "Don't worry, you won't have long to wait before they come to us." I looked at Kamenev. "See if you can get us another room. We're going to need it."

CHAPTER 26

Flannel pajamas are not just for old people. I don't care what anyone says. I've always loved the softness and warmth of the things. I also like it because I don't need a lot of blankets when I sleep. Irina likes a plain, long t-shirt. Who was I to argue?

I was dreaming about something that disappeared the second I heard the door burst open. I looked up to see three silhouettes with long hair push through the threshold. The light dazzled me a millisecond later as Irina, standing out of sight, turned it on and revealed three young women in maid outfits, fangs exposed. She grabbed the first assailant by the hair and put her face into the ground. She was to be the lucky one.

A heavier blonde woman leaped onto the bed and reached for me. I clapped the palm of my hand on her forehead and watched her skull steam and melt as she died screaming. The rest of her dissolved slowly until only a dark skeleton remained. A shame about the sheets. There was no cleaning that mess.

The third assailant had extremely long, curly hair. Her eyes looked left and right, not sure what to do. She hissed at Irina and took a quick step towards her. That was a mistake.

Harada came through the door and raised his pistol. It had a suppressor on it, and it made a loud spitting sound as he put one right between the eyes of the third maid from hell. It must have been one of the special bullets with my DNA because she melted fast.

I walked over to where Irina was holding down a black-haired maid with a fistful of hair. Her face was on the floor, and her arms thrashed. The small Russian lifted up her head and slammed her face back into the floor. "Stop moving!" she commanded.

Lowering myself to one knee, I looked at Irina. "Let her see me, please."

Irina turned her wrist, and the maid's glowing green eyes looked my way. She hissed but then stopped. I could see the fear in her eyes.

I pointed at the body on the bed, and the one Harada had killed. "Do you know who I am? Do you understand what happened here?"

"*Medusa's Son,*" she spat at me. "*You must die!*"

"And one day, I will," I said with a smile. "But not today, and certainly not by you. Claude Borges sent you, didn't he?"

She just glared at me, saying nothing. I glanced at Irina and she slammed her head into the floor, harder this time. "Answer!" Irina shouted.

"*Yes*," the poor creature hissed, whimpering.

"Claude Borges sent you here to die. Probably just gave you a room number and told you to kill the man in it. He didn't warn you about me or my team, did he?"

"*No.*"

"What is your name? Give me your full name, and you just might survive this."

"*Rosa. My name is Rosa Cortez*," she whispered, and I saw her humanity. I saw it in her eyes.

"Okay, Rosa. You have a very big choice to make." I sat down cross-legged and looked at her. "I know what you're going through. Hungry all the time, out of your mind with it. Right after you feed, you remember who you are and what you had, and then it's gone again. No matter how much you feed, it's never enough. Am I right?"

"*Yes!*" she cried, and I saw tears of blood gather in the corner of her eyes. "*Never enough.*"

"There is another way," I said, smiling at her. "The woman who is holding you down is Irina Kamenev. She was a vampire for twenty years. We were able to treat her, cure her. I'd like to do the same for you. There is a chance you'll die, but I don't think you've been infected for very long. I think you are going to survive." I got on both knees and lowered myself so I was looking at her. "Do you want what you had back? Do you want the thirst gone?"

"*Yes ... YES!*" she cried, red tears flowing onto the floor.

"It is not pleasant," Irina told her. "Every inch of your body hurts, and you pray for the devil to take you." She let the woman raise her head off the floor a few inches so they could see each other. Irina's large, dark eyes looked into hers. "When it is over, you have your life back. You will have memory of what you were. God help you. But it is worth it."

The woman's breathing became more regular, and she looked calmer. It was now or never. "Rosa, can my associate treat you? Will you let us help you?"

Her whole body sagged. "*Yes, help me. Please!*" she cried.

I looked up at Doctor Kimiko, who had entered the room, dressed and ready. "Is the room prepared, Doctor?"

She nodded. "It's ready. I just need Irina to get her there and into the restraints. After that, the treatment is fast, and she will be disinfected ... or die." Kimiko looked at the ground and crossed her arms on her chest. "She is in for a rough night."

I looked at Irina and then Rosa. "I'll see you on

the other side, Rosa. I think you're going to make it."

She didn't say anything as Irina hauled her up and got both arms behind her back. I could see the conflict on the petite Russian's face. Part of her wanted to kill Rosa, part of her was reliving her own experience. I felt for them both.

Backing up, careful not to touch any part of Kimiko's new patient, I watched Irina muscle her through the door and out of sight. Kimiko and Harada followed them, and he still had his gun out. Yakuza didn't take chances.

I walked into the hall and saw Kamenev standing there, a slight smile on his lips. "You were right, Walt. How did you know?"

Looking down the hall, I saw bleary-eyed guests poking their heads into the hall and scowling at us. I looked at the big Russian and winked. "I'll tell you in a minute, I have to do a little damage control for the hotel."

I walked past him and held up both hands to all the faces looking my way. "I'm so sorry! My girlfriend has a bit of a drinking problem, and she's suffered a bit of a relapse … but it's okay now. She's going to sleep it off. So sorry to have disturbed you."

There was grumbling, but gradually, the doors shut, and we were alone in the hall. Kamenev put a hand on my shoulder, "Come back to my room and have a drink with me, Walt. Tell me what you think is happening."

I grinned at him. "Is that because you want information or someone to drink with?"

He let out a belly laugh. "Both! I never know what you will say next, Walt. Come, let's talk."

CHAPTER 27

We walked into his big suite, and he looked over his shoulder. "Rum and Coke?" he asked as he strolled to the bar.

"Sure," I answered. It sounded like a good idea.

I heard the ice landing in glasses and the pouring of liquid as I sat down in a comfortable chair. My host finished pouring and mixing our drinks and came over to the seating area. He handed me my drink. I thanked him, and he sat down heavily in the chair opposite mine. "I really must ask ... how did you know they would try for you? How did you know that Borges would send them?"

I took a big drink and almost choked. There was a lot more rum in there than expected. I blinked quickly and cleared my throat. "It was something that Kimiko said and something you said. Two things that are a contradiction. Yet, both are true."

"Please, explain. I find this most interesting," Kamenev said with a smile.

"Well, Kimiko said that vampires are mindless, ravenous monsters. During a teleconference, you said they had a complex international system. That there was a hierarchy."

"I remember," he said.

"That got me thinking. I mean, I'd seen both. Irina was out of her mind with thirst, while that frightening old Spaniard, Pablo, he knew what he was doing. Then it came to me. The age of the vampires determined everything."

The Russian pointed a finger at me. "You think the older vampires are running things?"

"Yes, the old ones probably knock around the younger creatures." I took another drink and shuddered. That was a strong drink. "I figured that Borges was probably pretty high up in New York, so when Marie came back with her tail between her legs, babbling about Medusa's son, he'd send someone to deal with me. Someone expendable."

"And now one of these pawns belongs to us," Kamenev said, taking a swig of his beloved vodka.

"That's right, And I'm betting she's going to tell us everything we need to know and more."

He raised an eyebrow. "You think she'll tell us where they are?"

I gave him a big shrug. "We'll just have to see how cooperative she feels."

Our conversation was interrupted by a pounding on the door. "This is Martin Scott. Open up!"

Kamenev let out a sigh and shook his head as he made his way to the front door. I heard it open, and the Russian spoke. "Ah, Mister Scott. Please come in and tell us what is on your mind."

The manager was red-faced and walked into the middle of the room, glaring first at me and then back at Kamenev. "I've had complaints from guests about some loud disturbance in Mister Baranov's room. Something about a domestic dispute."

I laughed. I couldn't help it. "Oh, I told them my girlfriend had a bit of a drinking problem, but she was sleeping it off. I apologized to them. I guess that wasn't enough."

Scott snorted, "No, it wasn't enough. They also complained that they saw a man carrying a gun. What do you know about that?"

"Ah, that would be Harada. He had a pistol that he had to use. It wasn't really a domestic fight. Three vampires were sent to take me out." I smiled and spread my hands. "What can I tell you? They failed."

The manager looked at me with a frown and then turned back to Kamenev, who merely smiled. "It is true," the Russian confirmed.

Scott's face screwed up into that arrogant and stupid smile. "Again, with the vampire nonsense.

I can't believe Agent Boland is willing to accept this nonsense, *but I am not!*"

Kamenev looked at me. I sighed and stood, walking right up to the manager. "Well, seeing is believing. We caught one of them, and she's being treated right now. Would you like to see one?"

The color and that stupid smile ran away from his face. "You're joking."

I laughed. "I felt the same way until I saw my first. I can tell you this, Mister Manager man ... you *never* forget seeing your first vampire." I walked toward the door. "Follow me, and we'll see how you explain this one away."

CHAPTER 28

We got to the door, and I held up a hand to stop our progress and brought a finger to my lips to keep him quiet. "Irina, it's Walt. Please open the door," I whispered.

Ten seconds later, the door opened, and Irina smiled at me. It disappeared when she looked at the manager. "What do you want?" she asked.

I held up both hands to slow her down. "Checking on Rosa. Is she okay?"

She opened the door wider for us. "We are just about to start. This will not be pleasant."

I looked at the manager, whose eyes were darting around. He was uneasy, but it wasn't just fear. "Good, I think Mister Scott needs to see this," I said as we walked in.

Kimiko was standing beside a bed with the young woman restrained by straps on her arms and legs. Her long black hair was splayed out on the white pillow, and her eyes were still that unnatural glowing green. She was wearing a hospital gown that was white with small blue flowers. The most shocking thing was her mouth. It was wide, and teeth were everywhere. She moaned when she saw me. "*Medusa's Son, stay away!*" she hissed with that unnatural timbre.

"I'm not going to touch you, Rosa. We're going to try and help you." I looked at Kimiko. "Sorry to bother you. Had to be done."

"We are about to start the first phase of treatment," Kimiko explained, looking at the manager. "We have to boost her ability to recover, then we introduce the antigens necessary to destroy the virus."

"A ... a virus?" Scott mumbled. No trace of that stupid smile now. His eyes were riveted to the creature on the bed. I was right. He would never forget his first sighting of one of these things. He'd never look at the world the same way again.

"Yes," Kimiko explained. "It is a virus that has rewritten her DNA. She doesn't produce red blood cells anymore, so she gets it from her victims. We are attempting to destroy the virus." She slid her glasses higher on her nose and looked at the floor. "It is an extremely painful process, and there is no guarantee that she will survive."

"My God," Scott whispered. "Look at her. She really is a ... a."

"Vampire," Irina finished. "Yes. I was once just

like her. I will never forget." She looked at me and smiled, then turned toward the monster on the bed. "And I will never forgive."

"Starting phase one," Kimiko announced, and she put on some rubber gloves. She took a good-sized bag of blood and brought it to her patient. She held it up, and the creature started gorging herself on the bag. Blood spilled on the pillow and her chin. Eventually, she finished, and her eyes stopped glowing that odd green color.

The doctor took the empty bag away and found a new one. "Initiating phase two," she said quietly. Another bag of blood was in her hand, but this one was smaller.

"More blood?" Scott asked. "How is this different?"

I leaned closer and whispered to him. "This blood has antigens derived from mine. It doesn't have my DNA, or she'd just die. It does kill the virus, though."

The bag of blood came to Rosa's mouth, and she dug right in, biting through the membrane. Thirty seconds after she started, the bag was empty, and Kimiko took it away. She stood beside the bed and looked down at her patient, and waited.

Rosa's eyes bulged, and she gasped. A second later, an ear-splitting scream escaped her lips. She thrashed and pulled at her restraints. *"Dios mio!"* she screamed.

The manager had moved to press his back against the wall. He looked at me. "Uh, I think I've seen enough."

"She's going to go through this for the rest of the night. When it's over, she's going to be human again, or she'll be dead. There's no way to know," I explained, looking at the bed.

"I said I've seen enough," the manager growled. "I'm leaving."

I followed him out into the hallway. "So now you know we're telling you the truth, and Kamenev is not kidding when he tells you that this hotel has a vampire problem."

Scott looked at the carpet and nodded, frowning. "How long will it take you to deal with this 'problem?'"

"No way to know. I can tell you that if this woman survives, she can take us right to Claude Borges, and we will do the rest."

"Very well," the manager said and started walking away. He had a lot to process. It's not every day that you see a vampire.

"Oh, Mister Scott," I called down the hall. He turned to face me. "Keep your fingers crossed that she makes it. We don't have a 'plan B.' If this doesn't work, we're going to have to tear this hotel apart."

CHAPTER 29

I woke up in the morning. Alone. Irina did not come back to our room all night, but this didn't surprise me. I knew she had to see Rosa to the other side, whatever side that was. Her own rebirth must have been incredibly traumatic. Nobody gave her a choice, and she was alone when she went through it. She must have awakened in a cell, on the floor. I'll never forget how she came to us on the roof. The poor thing must have been desperate to find me, or anybody really.

I used the bathroom, cleaned up, dressed, and made my way to the room where they were treating Rosa. I considered whispering to see if she could hear me, but this wasn't a day for playing games. Even the ones Irina usually enjoyed. I rapped on the door with one finger and waited.

Kimiko came to the door, and she looked exhausted. She brought a finger to her lips to keep me quiet, and we crept into the hotel room. I wasn't sure what I'd see, but I didn't expect to see the two women sleeping peacefully. Irina was on her back, eyes closed, and Rosa was curled up like a child right beside her.

The doctor walked toward the door and gestured for me to follow. When we were in the hall, she spoke. "It was a rough night," Kimiko whispered. "Rosa was in a great deal of pain, and the noise she was making ... it was horrible."

"But ... she's going to be okay, right?"

Kimiko smiled and nodded. "Physically, I expect a complete and full recovery. Psychologically ...that's another story, I'm afraid."

"You're saying that physically she'll be okay, but she could have some mental health issues?"

"Of course," the doctor answered, stifling a yawn. "We have no idea what she's been through or seen. Irina needed a period of adjustment, remember?"

"I do." I paced around and thought about it for a moment. "Okay, why don't you get some sleep? We'll talk about when Rosa might be able to help us later."

The doctor placed a hand on my arm. "Thanks, Walt. But I must refuse. I will stay with my patient until she wakes. That is my duty. If there are any difficulties or hostility, Irina will protect me. I do thank you for your consideration."

I smiled at her. "You're awesome, Kimiko. I don't know what we'd do without you. Make sure you spend some time with Kim when you can. She's come a long way to be with you."

"Thanks for that, too." the doctor laughed and touched my cheek affectionately. "Back to work for me. Why don't you update Kamenev on Rosa's condition? It's safe to tell him she'll live now."

"Not a bad idea," I said to myself as I watched Kimiko go back into the hotel room housing two former vampires. It was incredible when you thought about it. I took out my phone and sent a quick text message. A moment later, I got a reply, and I marched to the elevator. It was time to get to work.

****

I walked into the manager's office, and Martin Scott was behind his desk. Kamenev and Agent Boland were sitting in the two chairs in front of him. I felt a little self-conscious because they were all in crisp suits, and I was in jeans and a sweater. I grabbed one of the smaller chairs and moved it to a point where I could see them, and they could see me.

"Glad you could make it, Mister Baranov," Scott drawled. "Do you have anything new to tell us?"

"Yes, I do. Some bad news and a plan of action if you're ready for it."

"I'm all ears," Agent Boland said with an easy smile. It was subtle, but it was clear he had little time for the manager. He was interested in anything that we had to say about vampires. It made me wonder if he'd seen some things others hadn't.

Kamenev just gave me a small smile and gestured with one hand for me to talk. It was my turn.

I took a breath and let it out. "Well, the young woman we captured last night will survive treatment. She's going to be normal ... or something that passes for normal."

"Will she be like Irina, Walt?" Kamenev asked. "Able to ... do unusual things?"

I could only shrug. "Too early to tell. Irina seems to be a bit of an anomaly. I doubt we'll ever be able to recreate the unique circumstances that gave her those incredible abilities. But you never know."

"I'm only interested in what you're going to do to rid my beautiful hotel of these ... these things," the manager said with a grimace.

"Sure. I get it." I clapped my hands on my knees and started. "Okay, when Rosa is able, we're going to ask her to take us to the vampires' lair."

"It's not in my hotel?" the manager asked.

"Your hotel is like a kind of train station for these things. It's a place they can hunt or come out of hiding to make their way through the city. When they're done, they go right back to the lair."

"We found a passage they have been using," Kamenev explained. "You used to have what Walt called a 'dumb waiter' from the days that the building was a law office. They use it to disappear after an attack or to go to the lower regions of the hotel."

"My hotel is a … a throughway for these things?"

"Yeah, they get what they need from one of your guests or one of your staff. If they don't get that, they go to the streets and use your hotel to get back to their lair. I'm certain of it."

"There's some truth to that," Agent Boland agreed. "I've been working with local law enforcement, and they've seen a big uptick in missing persons, and they're finding bodies with neck wounds. This hotel … it's the center of it all."

Martin Scott sat back in his chair. "Damn! I was hoping that the attack on your person was the end of the problem."

"No, that was the first salvo fired by Claude Borges. He did exactly what we expected. And now we will do exactly what he expects."

"What do you have in mind?" Kamenev asked.

I let out a sigh. "We have to suit up, go into the bowels of this hotel, and find out where the hell Borges could hide over a hundred vampires."

"And then?" Boland pressed.

"We deal with them."

Scott frowned at me. "You've got six members on your team. One is a doctor, and the other is just a young girl. You think you've got a chance against a hundred vampires?"

I smiled. "Might not be a hundred. Could be more. You're right that the doctor won't help us in a firefight, but you're dead wrong about Irina. She's the most dangerous member of our little band of mercenaries." I looked at my hands as I rubbed a palm with one thumb. "I'm hoping for a bit of a break. Something Borges won't expect."

Kamenev narrowed his eyes and pointed at me. "Why do I think you have another card you are waiting to play?"

"You know me too well, Comrade." I stood up and looked down at the three men. "I think the key to this whole thing is going to be Rosa. I think she's going to be the difference. Whether I'm wrong or I'm right, it's going to be a memorable confrontation. That much is certain."

CHAPTER 30

I walked through the bright atrium and onto the streets of New York's financial district. People in suits and business attire were on the move. They'd finished or skipped breakfast and were on their way to their offices. They marched like ants, not looking at me or anyone, really. They had a lot on their mind, and I couldn't help but notice that everyone seemed stressed.

Not me. No thanks. I didn't know what the future held or even how long I had on this earth. I did know that I wasn't going to spend it as a cog in a heartless business. It was a world of sales and purchases, and I didn't fit in. I didn't want to. With the money I'd made from my misadventures in Japan, there was no need to fear the future.

Except for this business with Claude Borges. That was worth fearing. I wondered what he was doing and why. Why would he turn so many people? Was he making a vampire army? It would explain why they were getting sloppy and leaving more evidence than in the past. There were too many noobs to supervise. At least, that was what I was hoping. When the time was right, that was something I could use to our advantage.

I found a couple of books at a newsstand I found interesting, settled on one and bought it. I put the paper bag under my arm and leaned into the wind. I ignored the people on the street ignoring me and made my way back to the hotel. The doorman greeted me, and I returned the salutation, stepping in out of the cold and into the lobby. I looked up at the big skylight and saw the different floors circle the building. It really was a lovely old hotel. I was hoping it would still be standing when we were done.

Breakfast seemed like a good idea, so I strolled into the restaurant. It wasn't busy, but I was surprised by some of their clientele. I saw Irina sitting with Kimiko's girlfriend, Kim. It took a moment to register, but I was fascinated to see that they were enjoying each other's company. A smile broke across my face, and I decided to leave well enough alone. I found a table for myself, and my server dropped off a menu and went to grab me a coffee.

I was joined by three hard cases. Sergei, Shaw, and the impassive Harada came to sit with me. "Well, well, well. If it isn't Medusa's Son," Shaw said with a wink.

"*Syn Meduzy*," Sergei echoed with a grin.

"Guys, enough," I chuckled. "It's weird enough as it is. Let's eat a big breakfast. I'll bet this place makes great eggs,"

"*Hai*," Harada said with a slight smile.

"So, now that we've captured and cured that poor girl, what's next?" Shaw asked.

"I was wondering same thing," Sergei asked. "When do we make our move?"

Our server came and took everyone's order. I was impressed with Harada's English. After our meals were requested and we had our coffee, I filled them in. "If Rosa's up for it, I'd like to suit up and have her take us to the lair."

"You have no idea what is down there waiting for us," Sergei said with a shake of his head. "Shaw told me the blonde parasite said there are over a hundred of the things."

"Yeah, I'm hoping that Rosa can give me a little more information. She's going to have a lot more to say when her recovery is over."

Shaw set down his coffee cup. "We do need more information. Might be a good idea to get Irina to ask."

I pointed at him. "Bingo! I mean, she's probably still terrified of me."

"No doubt," Sergei laughed. "She watched you melt someone with a touch. People tend to remember things like that."

We all laughed at his little joke. "Everyone is going to matter on this mission. We're going to need serious firepower. I looked at Shaw and Sergei. "You two will deliver everything we need and more. Might even get to shoot that crazy little rocket launcher of yours."

"That I would like to see," Sergei said with a grin.

I pointed at Harada. "You, my fine friend, will deliver the precision shooting I have seen you bring in the past."

"*Hai*, and protect Kimiko," Harada reminded us.

"Oh yes! I wouldn't ask you to shirk your duty to Kimiko or Oyabun."

"Oyabun?" Shaw asked.

"Head of the Yakuza. He's the boss," I explained as I took a quick sip of the hot coffee. "Yeah, have a relaxing morning and an afternoon nap, friends. I think we're in for a late night."

CHAPTER 31

I was sitting in a big chair, reading in our room, when Irina came in. She grinned and ran to me, happily jumping in my lap. "I have missed you!" she squealed and started kissing the top of my head.

"I missed you too," I laughed. "And you're squishing my book."

"Who cares about book? We are together again," she cheered.

"And that is a great thing. What you did for Rosa was also a great thing."

She leaned back and looked at me with wide eyes. "Oh, Walt. She went through such pain."

"So did you. Do you remember that?"

I felt her shudder. "I do. It was a nightmare, and I could not wake up."

I shook my head and looked into her eyes. "I'm so sorry that I wasn't there for you the way you were for Rosa."

Irina took my face with both hands and gave me

a gentle kiss on the lips. "You saved me. That is what I remember most. That is what I carry inside."

I looked down. I couldn't meet her in the eyes for this question. "You know what I have to ask you, right?"

"No," she whispered, looking down too. She knew.

"Is Rosa ready to help us?"

"*Da*, she is. But I am afraid for her."

I put a finger under her chin and tilted her head so she could see my eyes. "You have to know that we will protect her."

"I know. It will be very hard for her to go back there."

"You know that I wouldn't ask if we didn't need her."

She let out a sigh. "I know, Walt. I know."

"Well, get dressed and bring Rosa to your father's suite. We'll get a plan of action together, and we're going tonight."

She smiled. "What do I tell people who see me in the hotel? I will be dressed like an ancient fighter."

I shrugged. "Tell them you're going to a party."

"A costume party," she said, holding up her plumed helmet. "A weird costume party."

****

We were all gathered in Kamenev's suite, wearing all

our equipment and weaponry. My gladiator's helmet was on the seat beside me. We were waiting.

Everybody looked up as the door opened and Irina walked in wearing her battle gear, followed by a very timid Rosa. I stood up and smiled at her. "Welcome, Rosa. I'm so glad you're feeling better."

She smiled, but it disappeared when I offered my hand. "Is it safe?" she whispered.

"Yes," I chuckled. "Rosa, you are not infected anymore. You are no longer a vampire."

She took the hand I offered and laughed when nothing happened. Tears came to her eyes, and Irina wrapped a protective arm around her shoulders, steering her to an empty chair.

I glanced at the team and then turned back to Rosa. I dropped to one knee right in front of her. "Okay, Rosa. I have to ask you some things. Important things."

She nodded. "I will tell you what you need to know."

"Right. Here we go … Claude Borges is the one in charge, right? He is the oldest?"

"He is, and nobody is allowed to speak to him. He, his wife, and a few others decided who would feed and when."

My eyes widened. "By feed, do you mean go out and hunt New Yorkers?"

"Sometimes. Sometimes, they had bags of blood like you would find in a hospital."

I looked over my shoulder at Kimiko. She had raised an eyebrow and gave me a smirk. This was good news. We might be able to use that available blood for anyone she had a chance to treat.

I turned back to Rosa. "There is a group of older vampires that rule the younger ones. Do the older ones make vampires, too?"

She nodded, looking down at her lap. We were losing her to her memories, I could tell.

"Okay, Rosa. Do you remember how to get there?"

Her eyes looked up at me. "I will tell you."

I put a hand on her knee. "Actually, we were hoping you could take us there."

She brought a hand to her chest, and her eyes bulged. "*Dios mio, No!*"

"We will be with you—"

"There are too many! Too many," she finished in a whisper.

I wasn't sure how much longer she could take this. I decided to learn a little more. "Marie told us that there are about a hundred vampires working together."

Rosa stood up, shaking her head. "She lied. There are over three hundred monsters waiting for you!"

CHAPTER 32

I stood up, taking a few steps from Rosa. My eyes were wide, and my mind was whirling. I always figured that Marie Borges would not be completely forthcoming. I expected her to lie, to overstate their forces to intimidate us and scare us off. It never crossed my mind that she would try to make us overconfident and conceal their numbers. You had to give her credit. It was a smart move. Too bad it didn't work.

"Over three-hundred vampires," Kimiko whispered to herself. "That changes —"

"Nothing," I interrupted. "It changes nothing."

Kamenev looked at me and nodded, a grim smile on his face. "*Da*, Walt is correct. It changes nothing."

The doctor walked over to the bar and started pouring herself a stiff drink. "I do not know how you can have that point of view. We are a team of six people, with only five of the members having the ability to kill. I am merely here to treat the infected and the wounded. How can we ever hope to defeat that many?"

Irina knelt in front of Rosa, talking quietly to her. I looked at the rest of the team and saw the same uncertainty Kimiko was expressing. I gave them a small smile. "Nothing has changed because this is a problem that we absolutely have to deal with."

"Perhaps more soldiers, more firepower?" Sergei asked.

I shook my head. "While we find more soldiers, Borges makes more vampires. That also means more attacks. More people will die, and that will be our fault."

"Walt is on the right track," Kamenev said, joining Kimiko at the bar. "The more we delay, the less likely it is that we will succeed." He put some ice in a glass, and the vodka followed.

"Think about it," I said to everyone in the room. "Why would Borges, or anyone make so many vampires when secrecy used to be the priority?"

"He wants New York," Shaw said with a frown.

I pointed a finger at him. "That is the frightening truth. He knows about me, the treatment, and he's doing the only thing he can."

"He grows an army to overwhelm the city," Sergei growled.

"That's right," Shaw agreed. "He wants a legion of bodies, and he can cut them loose to grow his army. Maybe even double it."

Kamenev swirled the ice in his glass. "And if he succeeds, the other older vampires will take note. How long before we see it in other major cities? Los Angeles, Chicago, or perhaps even Moscow. This cannot be permitted."

I looked over to see Irina standing and leaning over. She was hugging Rosa, who was still seated in the chair. She walked over to me and gave me the news. "Rosa will come with us. I want to give her a helmet and a vest to protect her from bullets. She is to be right beside us on this mission."

I smiled at this small dynamo looking up at me. Our eyes met, and she eventually smiled, too. I put my hands on her shoulders. "Whatever you say. We'll keep Rosa safe."

"So, we're doing this?" Kimiko asked. "We're actually going to track down and deal with over three-hundred vampires?"

"Yes," Shaw said with a smirk.

Sergei stood up and looked at all of us. "Yes, we must."

Harada nodded his head and looked at Kimiko. "*Hai, Kyuketsuki* must die."

The doctor sighed and shrugged. "I guess this is where we earn our money."

I walked over to Rosa, still seated, and dropped to a knee again in front of her. "Don't worry, Rosa. I've got a plan. Irina has insisted we get you a helmet and body armor. We're going to see you safe."

"I will help you," Rosa said, sniffing back a tear. "They must be stopped. I don't want anyone else to suffer."

I smiled at her, "Cheer up Rosa. We're going to win the day, and you're not just going to help us. I think you're going to help everyone Borges has enslaved."

CHAPTER 33

Irina put the helmet on Rosa, who was already wearing body armor, and smiled as she helped her with the chin strap. "We will keep you safe. I swear it."

The rest of the team hefted their rifles, Harada had a hand on one of his holstered pistols, and the doctor was wearing her black coat and carried her matching medical bag. I put my helm on, and Irina did the same. We all started for the door, and Kamenev walked behind us as we left his spacious suite. We walked down the hall, and I heard the big Russian call to us. "Good hunting to you all!"

We raised a hand without looking back and made our way to the old elevator. "Where are we going, Rosa?" I asked.

"The basement. The old passage in the wall leads to the basement of this old hotel."

"You've been here before, haven't you?" I asked.

She took a shuddering breath. "Yes. My sister and I worked as cleaning staff in this hotel. We were both taken by Borges himself at the start of this madness."

We all got on the elevator, and we went down to the lobby. It was the middle of the night during the week, so we didn't see anyone but the hotel staff working the reception desk. I recognized the young woman named Candace. She stared at us, and I didn't blame her. Irina and I looked like Roman gladiators, and the three soldiers flanking Rosa and Kimiko looked like they were going to war. Probably because we were going to war.

Irina gave her a small wave, and Candace returned it with a laugh. We marched to the kitchen, and Rosa took us to a large pantry. Nobody said a word as she walked to an ordinary wall and pushed it. Nothing happened.

Rosa looked at Irina, who took a couple of steps to the wall and gave it a thump with one hand. A panel slipped up to show us the same passage we discovered on the same floor as the poor old woman who was killed.

"This is how they got up and down without being detected, right?" I asked.

Rosa nodded.

"Okay, where would they go from there, Rosa?"

The woman turned and looked at an old white fridge with patches of rust on the front. It was just sitting in the corner. She walked over and pointed at it. "Behind this thing is the way."

Irina took her cue and walked over to the old appliance. She put one hand near the top and easily toppled it over. Sure enough, there was a hole in the corner that was almost as large as the fridge.

Shaw walked over, pulled out a small, powerful flashlight, and shined it in the hole. "This thing opens up pretty wide and goes down into something even bigger. It's rough cement to start, then I see tiles everywhere. What the hell is this?"

Kimiko had her phone in her hand. "I believe this may lead to some kind of service tunnel. Perhaps to maintain some part of New York City's famed subway system?"

Shaw looked over her shoulder and nodded. "The Fulton Street station isn't too far from here. I just can't believe this tunnel is right here, and nobody knows about it."

"This city's subway system is hundreds of years old," I explained. "It really shouldn't surprise us if there are parts of the transportation system that have been abandoned and eventually forgotten."

"This could allow Borges and his army to move around the city without being detected," Sergei observed.

I saw Irina walk up to Rosa and put an arm

around her. Rosa sniffed back some tears and reached for the hand Irina had placed on her shoulder. She gave it a squeeze and shook her head. "I don't know if I can do this," she sobbed.

"Rosa, I want you to think of the others. The ones that Borges enslaved and the ones he will turn. Can you do it for them? You just have to show us the way. That's all."

"Maria," she sniffed. "My sister Maria is still down there. If I take you to her, can you help her?" She looked at me, and her eyes were desperate.

I looked at the doctor, who gave me a solemn nod. I looked back at the poor woman who was crying. "We can help her. If she lets us, Rosa."

CHAPTER 34

Shaw tossed me an extra flashlight, and I turned to the tunnel in the corner. My thumb pressed the rubber button, and the light tore through the darkness. My first couple of steps were tentative as the ground was uneven and rocky.

It soon smoothed out, and descent was easier. My flashlight showed a groove as wide as a foot worn into the dirt and stone. How long had vampires been using this tunnel, and how many?

I stepped out of the long, descending tunnel into a much larger void. Smooth cement greeted my boots, and the light reflected off the white ceramic tiles. Turning back to the tunnel, I shone the light into the opening to help the rest of the team.

Irina popped out, using her arm to shield her eyes from my light. Rosa, then Kimiko came next. Harada emerged with a pistol in his hand, followed by the two soldiers. I noticed the professionals had their fingers beside the trigger, not on it. Safe, but ready.

I took the point and moved my flashlight in the gloom. Irina was on my left; Kimiko and our guide were being shadowed by Harada and his watchful eye. I could hear Sergei and Shaw following us. The two soldiers watched our tail.

I felt Irina grab my arm and stop moving. I could feel the urgency in her grip. I looked at her, only to see her silently crank the crossbow and load it with a bolt. That confirmed it.

"What do you smell, babe?" I asked.

"Death."

I put a hand on her shoulder and whispered into her ear. "What flavor?"

She took a slow breath in through her nose. "A body, blood ... and a vampire."

Shaw came up beside us. "We can use our night vision goggles and take them out."

Irina smiled. "I have my own night vision." She looked at me. "Turn off light, please."

I killed the flashlight, and Shaw did the same. The darkness was absolute. I couldn't see a thing. "This needs to be quiet," I whispered into the black. I felt her take my hand and guide it to her crossbow.

"Hold this one minute," she whispered back.

The team stood still in the black. Nothing to see. The only sound was breathing. Ten seconds later, we heard the sound of steel sliding on steel and a thump as something hit the ground and rolled.

"It is done. Come!" Irina called to us. Shaw and I fired up the flashlights, and the whole party started walking in the direction of her voice. My flashlight fell on a head on the floor that faced away from us. The severed head of a vampire. Shaw's light revealed Irina, swords drawn, standing over the rest of the body. She was getting good with those things.

The doctor rushed up to another person lying on the ground, black bag in hand. I walked toward her, shining the light on her patient. I needn't have bothered. She looked up at me and shook her head. "Too late," she whispered.

The light revealed a teen, a young girl with curly blonde hair, a nose piercing, and blue eyes that stared into the great hereafter. The neck wound and the stare made it clear she was dead. Her clothes were old, worn, and too large. She was probably a street kid, but that didn't define her anymore. She was somebody's daughter. She wasn't a victim of the big city but one of a maniacal vampire's creatures. We couldn't save her, but I hoped she would be the last.

I put a hand on the doctor's shoulder. It was condolence and gratitude. Moving over to Shaw and Sergei, I looked at the vampire Irina had dispatched. They were examining the head.

"Looks young. New," Shaw observed.

Sergei turned it with his boot. "*Da*, not old at all."

I went to one knee for a better look at what they were describing. My own light illuminated the face, and it came into focus for me. The eyes were rolled back into the head, but I saw what they meant. Its skin was flawless, and long, reddish hair framed the face. The wide-open mouth had fangs, but the mouth was feminine and had full lips. It probably wasn't much older than its victim.

"This is not permitted," Rosa whispered, looking down at the head.

"Borges doesn't let them feed without his say-so, right?" I asked.

"Yes," she answered, bringing a hand to her eyes. "He usually provides bags of blood or a live victim. It was horrible to watch. I hated it."

I turned away from her and looked at Irina. "I doubt they came from the Beekman Hotel. Neither is dressed for that place. Any idea where they came from?"

I saw her face glowing in the artificial light, take a deep breath, and look around in the larger chamber. She started walking away, and I saw her beckon for me to follow. She stopped and pointed at a tunnel that looked just like the one we descended.

"Now, where does that go?" I wondered aloud.

"It goes up to an alley a block from the hotel," Rosa called to me. "I have used it."

"Look at this!" Shaw called, pointing with a hand at what his flashlight was revealing. Spelled with black tiles covered in dust were the words, "Fulton Street."

"This is definitely part of a subway system that was either abandoned or never completed," I concluded.

"Yes," Kimiko agreed. "And if they have access to the subway system and there are tunnels going up to the surface, these things can go anywhere in the city."

"Great. Borges has over three hundred vampires, and he can get them anywhere he wants. I'll bet he is careful to get his victims from random places to keep the authorities from understanding what's really going on."

"This must stop," Sergei muttered.

I put a hand on his shoulder. "And it stops tonight."

CHAPTER 35

Rosa took us further down the large chamber, and it narrowed until it was just a track, rusty and covered in dust. "We are getting close," she whispered. "Very close."

"Kill the lights," I said as I turned off my own flashlight.

"We're in the dark here," Shaw pointed out.

"I will walk you closer," Irina said. "I can see. It is not far."

We formed a line, one in front of the other, and inched through the darkness. Nobody said a word. Stealth was everything, and it wasn't easy walking down the subway track. The railway ties were uneven and hard to predict. Our patience was rewarded when we saw a dull glow further down the track.

"Be careful. We are almost there," Rosa hissed.

She wasn't kidding. Just a few more steps, and we were looking into a much larger chamber with a couple of ancient streetcars. The relics were covered in dust, and there was a pile of rubble in the center of the big chamber. I could see three openings like the one we followed at the far side of the massive room. A few lanterns burned in various locations and there were people everywhere. Well, they used to be people. Now, they were predators.

I saw movement in one of the old subway cars, and a tall man with medium-length dark hair started walking up the pile of rubble. He wore a dusty suit and had a staff that gave him a regal air like Moses climbing to address his people. I couldn't be sure from his profile, but when he turned our way, I knew. "Claude Borges," I whispered to the team.

He was followed by about a dozen vampires that were carrying bags of blood, and a couple of them were muscling a pair of portly businessmen in suits to the top of the pile. Marie Borges was one of Claude's inner circle, and she was still wearing the flashy red dress. I saw her snarl and slap one of the men, almost unconscious. Charming.

We saw the vampires all turn and crowd the big pile of rubble, and Borges had his minions throw the bags of blood to the crowding vampires. They all piled on the bags, pushing each other and gorging on the contents. It was unpleasant to watch, and then it got worse. Borges pulled a large, evil-looking knife and grabbed one of the businessmen. He slashed him across the chest and threw him to the snarling crowd. He tossed the knife to Marie and she happily did the same to the other man.

The crowd buried the poor men from our sight and I was glad for that. I did get to watch Marie and Claude Borges holding hands, grins on their faces from what they did to their victims. The mob started chanting their names and cheering. They were excited for the next act. I suspected what was coming next, but it didn't make it any easier.

Three teenagers, street kids in loose-fitting garments, were drawn screaming to the top of the large mound by more of Borge's minions. I numbered his inner circle at just over twenty. Like him, they looked old. The king of the vampires bit the poor teens on the neck, and as soon as he was done, he'd fling them to the waiting hands of his crew. They were carried to the old railcars to recover or die out of sight. It was horrible, and it lit a fire in my gut.

This was why I accepted this job, and I came to New York. To stop this and help those kids get right or die trying. I waved at everyone on the team and pointed in the direction we came. We'd seen enough.

Stumbling down the tunnel in the dark, we eventually came to where we started. "Thoughts?" I announced to the team as Shaw and Sergei fired up their flashlights in the old Subway station.

"There are too many," Kimiko said. "Definitely over three hundred vampire soldiers."

"Borges inner circle, how dangerous are they?" Shaw asked.

"As strong as Irina?" Sergei wondered. "We cannot deal with that kind of power."

"No," Kimiko replied. "Those infected are slightly stronger than a normal human being with similar size. Irina's strength was a freak event that was somehow caused by her transition. We still don't understand it."

Shaw shook his head. "If we go right at them, it's going to get bloody. I think we can win the day, but everybody dies. Everybody."

"Unacceptable," I said, looking down. "I didn't come here to kill every vampire in New York. I came to help as many as I can, and wading into a room full of infected people, spraying bullets is not an option."

Irina walked up to me. "I know that look on your face. You have a plan, *Nyet*?"

"Yes," I answered and put my hands on her shoulders, looking down into those deep, dark, liquid eyes. I smiled at her. "You're not going to like it." I laughed and looked at the others. "None of you are going to like it."

CHAPTER 36

I talked and talked in the gloom of the old subway station. I threw a few lame jokes in there, but nobody laughed. They listened, and they didn't say anything. Their faces did the talking. Eyes grew wider and then hostile. I saw arms crossed on chests and a few glares sent my way. Sometimes, they would look at each other and shake their heads, but they didn't say a word. Not one of them looked impressed.

When I finished, I clapped my hands together and smiled. "Any questions? Concerns?"

"Yes," Doctor Kimiko said with a tilt of her head. "When did you completely lose your mind?"

"I know it seems extreme—"

"Insane," she interrupted. "It seems insane."

"Okay, I get why you would say that." I looked at the others. "And you? How are the rest of you with this?"

"I do not like plan," Sergei mumbled, looking at his boots.

"I'm with you, Comrade," Shaw agreed. "You're taking all our advantages and gambling them away on a hunch, Walt."

"I wouldn't call it a hunch," I said with a shrug. "I think it's the best way to go about this. I think that it's a perfect way of beating Claude Borges at his own game."

"Or give him what he wants," Irina said with a glare that would peel paint.

I pointed at her. "It's sure going to seem that way."

"No," Harada grunted. "Too much danger."

Smiling at my old friend from Japan, I nodded. "There is a lot of danger. Coming right at them is dangerous for everyone. This plan has a real chance of succeeding if everyone does their job."

"It could also fail spectacularly, Walt," Shaw said, shaking his head. "Could be the end of the division, really."

"I know where you're coming from, I really do. I had my doubts when it first came to me, but the more I watched the vampires, the more I believed in it." I smiled. "I do believe in the plan. But really, I believe in you. All of you."

They all looked at me, blinking. "Really?" Shaw snorted. "That's it?"

"No, really!" I chuckled. "This is a team of

specialists, and there will never be another one like it. I couldn't even consider trying this if you didn't have my back."

Irina walked to me and looked up. She was so petite it was easy to forget the power in that body. I never underestimated the strength of her character. "I don't want to lose you," she whispered.

I embraced her and felt her melt into me. "You won't." We parted, and I looked at the team. "All this is academic. There's only one person who needs to agree." I walked up to Doctor Kimiko and looked at her. "So what about it, old friend? Are you up for it?"

She rolled her eyes and looked away from me, folding her arms on her chest. She paced for a moment and stopped. She turned to face me and shrugged. "Look, I see what you're trying to do, and I have to say, it's a brilliant strategy. But it all depends on one thing that is not certain. How can you hang everything on such a gamble?"

I walked to her with a smile. "See, that's just it. I don't think it is a gamble. I think it's a certainty, and it all comes down to timing." I turned and looked at Irina. "Do you think you can hold up your end of the plan?"

She scowled at me. "Of course I can. Don't be stupid."

The whole team laughed in the poorly-lit station

and it echoed off the tiles. I turned back to Kimiko. "Well, Doc, it's down to you. Are you up for it?"

She let out a sigh and glared at me. "You better be right." She pointed a finger at Irina. "You too!"

"So you'll do it?" I asked with a grin.

"You are insane, do you know that?" she asked.

"Is that agreement?"

"Yes, you are insane, and yes … I'll do it."

"Great!" I cheered. "Let's show the world what the Medusa Division can do."

CHAPTER 37

We walked down the tunnel toward the glow of the massive chamber. Aside from the occasional stumble on the railway ties, we were making good time. Too good. "We've got to slow down, give the others time," I said in the darkness.

I reduced my pace accordingly and we eventually saw more light and the wide opening to Claude Borges's unholy assemblage. I looked over my shoulder at my partner. "This is it. Are you ready?"

I saw the plumed helmet nod and her grip tighten on the crossbow. She was as ready as she'd ever be. It was showtime.

Setting down my Medusa-faced shield, shifting the titanium mace to my left hand. I depressed the button and felt the stab of the needles into my palm and then their removal. It wasn't too painful as my adrenaline was running on high. I put it back in my right hand and pressed the button again. After the stab of the needles, I looked down at the head of the weapon and saw it dripping with blood. Good.

"Here we go," I said to my partner, hefting the shield in my left hand. "Keep behind me and make sure they see that crossbow." I started running, and I saw Borges and his entourage standing on the pile of rubble, their altar. They were throwing the bags of blood again. I wondered if the teenagers they bit earlier were in the crowd. I hoped not.

A few vampires turned and reached out for us, pressing forward. I shouted and swung the mace hard, and the blood that had pooled on the head spread in a large arc, hitting the faces of the vampires who turned to face me when I yelled. They screamed and clawed at their faces as the skin fell away, and they died. A crossbow bolt flew past my shoulder and struck a vampire in the head. It, too, melted away quickly.

Another swing brought death to the vampires behind the first victims. I looked up to see I'd gotten the attention of the head vampire himself. He was pointing a clawed finger at me and saying something to the vampires around him. Great!

"CLAUDE BORGES!" I screamed with everything I had, and the whole room went silent. I pointed my mace at him. "I am Medusa's Son, and you know who this woman is and what she can do."

My bodyguard stepped forward, and she raised her crossbow while her dark eyes glared through the fancy, plumed helmet. The vampires hissed and withdrew, holding their hands up for protection. They opened a path right to the big mound in the center of the room and the older vampires who looked down at us. Yes, they knew who I was. Kamenev had not underestimated the power of a legend. Time to live up to the hype.

Borges took a couple of steps toward us, his ghastly mouth screwed into what passed as a smile. *"Yes, I know of you. Medusa's Son, the motherless brat from Croatia who killed so many of our kind in Japan."* His voice was eerie, hollow, and rasped from deep in his lungs. *"And now you have come for us? Is that right?"*

"It is," I answered. "But it doesn't have to be. I guarantee you that more vampires *will* die here today. I can also promise that some vampires will walk out of this chamber and live."

Borges glared at me and gestured to some of his followers who trained rifles on us. This was not part of the plan. If they shot first and asked questions later, this was not going to work. At least, I wouldn't be around to see it.

Marie Borges stepped forward in her glamorous red dress and sneered at us. *"What do you and your demon girl think you can do against all of us?"* she snarled with that unearthly voice.

I laughed. "Kill you all! But that is not why I

came. I came to talk to you about something better. Something we can both live with."

Claude and Marie Borges looked at each other, frowning. He looked back at me. *"And why do you offer any compromise when you believe that you can defeat us? This makes no sense."*

I laughed and started walking forward. "I know that many of the vampires in this lair were recently turned. I also know that most didn't have a choice. I would bargain their lives for yours. You get to live, and so do they."

He held up a hand to stop our progress. *"That's close enough!"* he barked. He walked back to the top of the mound and gestured for his minions to lower their guns. They did, and I breathed a little easier. *"Why would you do me this great, benevolent favor? What is in it for you?"*

I shrugged. "I'm paid to solve vampire problems. I'm not paid for each vampire killed. It was never my choice to carry DNA that kills vampires. We can treat the people recently infected while you slip away. I get paid, and you live. Everybody wins." I pressed the button on the mace, and blood oozed out of the weapon, and I pointed it at the vampires starting to press in. "Or everybody dies."

The crowd of snarling things pulled back when they saw the blood on my mace. They saw what I did to the vampires who blocked our entrance. They wanted me dead, but their overwhelming sense of self-preservation prevented them from going for it.

Claude Borges glared at me, gauging my answer. He beckoned with his hand, "*Come closer, Medusa's Son. I would look upon the legend my people fear and his demon bride. I think you're just a boy.*"

I laughed as I moved forward. "A boy? I left a lot of corpses in Japan, and I can tell you that they knew different ... before they died at my touch."

The vampires hissed at that statement, and hatred radiated throughout the room. I glanced to my left and saw my partner's hands clutching the crossbow a little tighter. She only had to make it a little longer. We were almost there.

Marie Borges came close to her husband and ran a hand through her blonde hair to move it out of her face. She placed a hand on her husband's shoulder. Her eyes glowed green as she glared at us. She frowned as she whispered in his ear.

He took a step closer and hissed. "*Remove those helmets. I would look upon your face to see the veracity of these claims.*"

Oh crap! This was not part of the plan.

I took a breath, then lifted off my gladiator's helmet, looking the old vampire right in the eye. "Is this what you want?"

Marie pointed at us and spoke up. *"And her! I would see her again after what she did to me in that alley."* She shook a fist at us. In fairness, Irina did beat the stuffing out of her. It was the kind of thing nobody could be expected to forget. A shame that I did!

I leaned to my left and whispered, "Take it off … you have to."

The crossbow was set on the ground, and the plumed helmet was removed. Long, dark hair cascaded down, and she looked up at the old monsters. I saw Marie Borges take a step back.

She grabbed her husband's shoulder with one hand and pointed an accusing finger with the other. *"Claude, that's … that's NOT her!"*

"Is this a part of the plan, Walt?" Kimiko whispered, glaring at me.

"Yes, Doctor," I whispered with a smile. "Get ready to run!"

CHAPTER 38

I heard the familiar sound of steel sliding on steel, and Claude Borges's eyes bulged as his head left his body. Marie recoiled as blood spurted all over her, and I saw Irina standing behind them without her helmet. She had her two swords in each hand, and she kicked what was left of Claude Borges twenty feet into the astonished crowd of monsters.

His vampire deputies quickly trained their guns on the young Russian woman but never got a chance to fire. Sergei, Shaw, and Harada came out of the tunnels behind the mound of rubble, and their weapons were drawn and blazing.

The Russian soldier sprayed bullets into the older vampires while Harada fired with pinpoint accuracy with his pistols. While the old guard recoiled under their attack, Irina swung her sword and instantly removed Marie's blonde head from her body.

"Come on, Kimiko!" I shouted, dropping my shield and grabbing her hand, pulling her forward toward Irina. We were out of time.

Shaw took a knee and lifted a green pipe that looked like a tiny bazooka on his shoulder. He looked down the sights, pulled the trigger, and his M72 Rocket Launcher sent a missile arcing toward the ceiling. It exploded with a deafening impact. Large chunks of the cement above us fell on the younger vampires, driving them back from the large mound. That would give us the time we needed to dispatch the old guard and keep the young ones out of the fight.

I heard shouting and saw Sergei with one of the older vampires on top of him, clawing at his face. I ran to help, but Shaw was there first. A couple of shots from his rifle, and it was over. "Stay with him!" I shouted and ran to the back of the mound, looking at the tunnels.

Turning to look back, I saw Harada and Irina fighting hard. The tough Japanese gangster was letting the bullets fly and was hitting everything he aimed for. Irina … she was just *magnificent*. She put the swords away and was pounding any vampires stupid enough to get close to her. A punch would send them flying backwards. A kick would send them back much further.

Looking in the tunnels, I found what we needed. I ran to her and sank to one knee. "Rosa, it's now or never. Will you come with me?" I held out both hands for her.

The poor woman trembled and reached for my hands. I helped her leave the tunnel, then turned and grabbed Doctor Kimiko's black bag. We would need it.

"*Dios mio!*" she whimpered as we started up the mound.

"Claude Borges and his wife are dead," I assured her. "We're almost there. You can do this, Rosa!"

It felt like an eternity before we made the top of the mound. Irina had drawn her swords, and I saw Harada reload his pistols in a flash. Shaw was firing bursts of the special ammunition, and Sergei was on his feet but missing an eye. This had to stop *now*!

"Irina, we need your voice!" I shouted at the small girl as she lopped the head off a gigantic old vampire. The last of the old guard was dead, and only the youngsters remained.

She looked at me and gave a quick nod. She turned and screamed at the crowd with an unnatural volume. "AHHHHH! THAT IS *ENOUGH!*" Her voice poured out of her like thunder, startling everyone in the large chamber.

Everyone stopped to look at the source of this incredible noise. I smiled at her and helped Rosa move forward. "You know who I am!" I shouted to the seething monsters. "Some of you know who this is. This is Rosa. She was just like you, and we helped her.

We can treat you. You don't have to hunger anymore!"

The vampires stared at Rosa and looked at each other. "It is true," she said with a shaking voice that echoed in the silence. "I was like you. Just like you." She scanned the crowd, tearing up. "Maria! Where are you, Maria?"

A vampire with long, black hair covered in dirt stepped forward from the crowd, hissing. She limped, and she was dressed in a simple black dress that a maid would wear. "*Rosa!*" she hissed as blood dripped from her chin.

"Maria!" she cried. "Please let us help you, *hermana!*"

I handed the black bag to Kimiko, and she dug for what she would need.

Rosa beckoned for her to come closer, but the fear was too great. She pointed at me and shook her head. I looked at Irina, and she knew what needed to be done.

Irina sheathed her swords and walked toward the young vampire woman. She stopped and held out her hand.

"Irina was like you, too," I explained to all of them as I took a few steps back from Kimiko. "I'm telling you … we can help you get better. You don't have to die here today. Your old life is just waiting for you!"

Maria looked at Irina's hand skeptically but reached out slowly and took it. Irina turned and gently moved the poor creature closer to Kimiko. The doctor spoke to her but was sure that the rest of the crowd could hear. "This is a painful treatment. I cannot lie. But it does kill the infection. You will be free of this curse."

Kimiko loaded a syringe and injected the contents into the wide-eyed Maria while Rosa held her hand. She screamed and dropped to her knees. The crowd of young vampires hissed and were restless, but their eyes stayed on the scene in front of them.

"How are we doing, Doc?" I said under my breath.

"I cannot say for sure," Kimiko whispered back. "But ... I think I can see some changes already."

"Stand her up," I whispered.

The doctor looked at me. "Walt, she's in a lot of pain."

"They all are," I said, pointing at the crowd of milling vampires with my mace. "They need to see this."

Kimiko and Rosa helped the suffering Maria to her feet, and she looked at the crowd. I could hear the vampires gasping, a strange, hollow hissing. It wasn't hard to see why. Maria's eyes and mouth had changed, and even though her face was contorted with pain, she was human. Obviously human.

"You see! Do you see this?" I called to the horde. "This is waiting for you. If you want your old life back, let us help you." I nodded at Irina, and she drew her swords again. I heard the soldiers ram a clip into their rifles, and Harada moved a bullet into the chamber of his pistol. I pointed to the deadly trio with my mace, "Or you can die right here, right now. What's it going to be?"

Time stood still, and the silence was awkward. A young woman, one of the street kids we had seen Borges turn, took a couple of steps forward, removing herself from the crowd. "*Help me!*" she hissed. "*Please … help me!*" and tears of blood ran down her face.

More vampires stepped forward, one after the other, asking for help. Shaw sidled up to me and shook his head. "I don't believe it … you actually pulled this off."

I grinned at him. "No, Green Beret. The Medusa Division did this. All of us."

CHAPTER 39

The next few hours were amazing. Shaw went up to street level and contacted Kamenev, letting him know our status. The tough old Russian must have made some calls of his own because medical staff and police officers soon met Shaw, and he walked them down the tunnels to the big chamber to help.

As long as I live and breathe, I will never forget the look on the faces of the paramedics and New York's finest. These experienced first responders just froze, seeing the mass of vampires milling around at the bottom of the mound. The shock, the horror, and the complete understanding that passed over their faces happened in a heartbeat.

Still, consummate professionals that they were, they snapped into action, and Kimiko stood and led the charge. The doctor had the vampires form something of a line, and paramedics monitored the vitals and health of the vampires who had just been treated. They thrashed in pain, but it was never for very long. Borges had been very busy and these poor creatures were very recently made. The upside was that the pain wasn't as severe or prolonged.

The police officers were just fantastic. They were there to help the medical staff when they needed a helping hand and talk to anyone who was recovering from Kimiko's cure. Sometimes, it was just being a shoulder to cry on, and other times, they were taking notes. They were professional and kind. They were helping, listening, and investigating.

I heard a voice from just behind me. "Looks like we really do have a vampire problem, and there's definitely more than one."

Agent Boland was standing there in his crisp grey suit and smiling. He was looking at the vampires still waiting for treatment. I couldn't help but laugh. "Good to see you, Agent Boland," I said, offering a hand.

He reached out and shook it with a strong grip, then pointed at the monsters waiting their turn to be saved. "A pleasure to be here. This explains a lot of the loose ends we've been dealing with over the last six months."

"I'll bet."

"What's next for you, Walt?" he asked.

I took in a breath and let it out in a big sigh, looking around the big chamber. "I think it's time my team had a shower and some rest. Then I'm going to buy them some drinks and a snack." I looked at the agent with a smirk. "I was wondering if you could help me with one loose end in a few hours."

Boland smiled and looked back at the vampires being treated. "Pretty sure I know exactly what you're talking about." He handed me his card and looked back at all the activity in the chamber. "It would be my pleasure. Just give me a call."

****

Six hours later, we were washed, rested, and dressed to fit in at the Beekman's famous bar. It was called "The Bar Room," and it was the perfect place to celebrate. The black and white tiles on the floor were timeless, and the mirrors on either wall made it seem more spacious than it really was. We had taken a couple of round-topped tables by the very end of the bar. Kamenev sat at one with Harada and Kimiko, while Irina and I took the other right beside them. Sergei and Shaw were sitting on the tall, leather topped stools at the bar. They had turned to face us and had a drink in their hands. Everyone did.

I was wearing the dark gray suit, the only one I owned, and Irina was spectacular in her silver and black dress. Her matching silver earrings and necklace gleamed in the low lights of the place, and she let her long, dark hair spill down her back. She was stunning, and I found it hard to look away from her.

Shaw and Sergei were dressed in their military finery. They were something to see, the Green Beret and the Spetsnaz soldiers, side by side. Sergei was sporting a black leather patch to hide the dressing where his left eye used to be. He didn't care, and it only made him more dashing.

Kamenev and Harada sported black suits and ties, while Kimiko was wearing a lovely ivory dress. It was long and off one shoulder and contrasted nicely with her black hair and the suits of her escorts.

Kimiko's eyes widened, and she stood up to run to her partner, Kim Rourke, as she walked into the bar. The tall, pale redhead was wearing a deep blue dress that brought out her eyes, and she embraced the shorter Kimiko tenderly. They talked and gave each other a gentle kiss. They came to join us and greetings were exchanged.

"Okay," I said to everyone. "We're all here. Now it's a party!"

CHAPTER 40

Kamenev raised a hand. "So please, tell me how you dealt with this problem. I am interested to know what you faced and how you solved it."

All heads turned to me, and I took a breath and stood out of my chair to be seen and heard. "Okay, we found a chamber with over three hundred vampires, and it was a pretty awful scene. Claude Borges and his wife, Marie, were the obvious rulers in that lair, and he had about twenty old vampires working for him."

"That means almost three-hundred vampires were created by Borges and his wife? Extraordinary," Kamenev said with a shake of his head.

"I know, right?" I agreed. "The Borges were probably living under the radar for years, using the Beekman Hotel as a way to move around the city and hunt. They were obviously successful, so why change? Why make so many vampires?"

"To overwhelm the city with sheer numbers," Sergei answered. "Like Napoleon's vast number of untrained troops."

"That's exactly right," I said, pointing at him. "When they heard about me and that there was a cure for vampirism, they made a decision."

"They started making vampires. Lots of them," Kimiko suggested.

"Yes." I rolled my eyes and shook my head. "The Borges created a pretty sizable force, but it wasn't by choice, and they had no loyalty to the couple."

"There is a logic to that thinking," Kamenev agreed. "You sought to cut the head off the snake?"

"Yes, but that alone wouldn't do it. The poor things are so crazy with hunger, that thirst for blood … they needed a way out."

"Rosa," Shaw said, pointing at me with his glass. "That's why you needed Rosa to come with us."

I pointed my glass back at the Green Beret. "Oh, I needed her to show me where the Borges were holed up, but yeah … I needed their army to see that they didn't have to fight us, and they didn't have to fight anyone. They needed a way out, and I hoped that seeing Rosa would convince them."

Kamenev looked down into his glass and asked a question. "Out of curiosity, what would you have done if they were not convinced and wanted to destroy you?"

"Kill them all," I said and took a drink. Nobody

said anything as it sunk in how horrible that would have been. Three-hundred souls needlessly killed.

"That would be ... unfortunate," Kamenev agreed. "How did you proceed, knowing all this?"

"Ah," I said, snorting a laugh. I was feeling the effects of the alcohol. "This is where we disagreed. I had to pull rank on this one."

The team smiled, and I saw Kimiko look at Kim and roll her eyes. "He can be very stubborn," she told the redhead.

"Yes, it is most annoying," Irina agreed.

"Hey, I'm right here!" I said, laughing.

"Please, I must know ... what was the plan?" Kamenev pressed.

"Right ... okay. Knowing that they used tunnels to get to street level, I asked Irina to take the team members with guns and sniff out the tunnel that would get them behind Borges and his entourage to take them out." I smiled at them all, "They didn't like that plan."

"No, we did not." Irina agreed.

"*Hai*, dangerous plan," Harada said with a frown.

"Yet, a successful one," I said, pointing at my friend from Japan.

"What were you and Kimiko doing while they were looking for this tunnel?" Kamenev asked.

"Right, well ... we needed a big distraction so

that our deadliest members could get close to Claude and Marie and ...do what needed doing," I explained.

Kamenev raised an eyebrow. "So, you let them see you?"

"Worse," Kimiko growled. "He had me wear Irina's helmet and carry her crossbow, and yes ... we ran right into that viper's nest."

The big Russian took a breath and let out a big sigh. "Dividing the team like that ... I can see why they were reluctant."

"See, I just don't look at it that way." I took a drink and looked at the floor. "You just know that Irina has the ability to find that tunnel, and there's no doubt that if these soldiers could get behind Borges, it was game over." I pointed at Kimiko. "I don't know what you're complaining about, Doc. You were amazing with that crossbow. That bolt you let go just missed my head and nailed that vampire in front of me right between the eyes. I mean, wow! It was a great shot."

"It was a total accident," Kimiko answered and laughed as she took a drink. "I did not mean to shoot that crossbow at all."

My mouth hung open, and I stared at her. "Wait, what? That arrow went right over my shoulder. You didn't aim and shoot that thing?"

She shrugged and looked at the floor. "I was running, and I had no idea that the trigger was so sensitive. I am sorry, Walt. I did not mean to shoot that arrow or any arrow."

Maybe it was the alcohol or the look on my face, but the whole team started laughing. Sergei and Shaw were busting a gut, the Russian pounding the bar with a hand while Shaw covered his eyes with one hand. Harada was quiet in his laughter, but I'd never seen him smile like that. Irina had wrapped both her hands around her belly, and her eyes were closed as she cackled away.

Kimiko grinned as her partner, red in the face, laughed and put her head in her hands. "I am sorry, Walt. It is the truth."

"Okay, fine," I said, holding up both hands. "To be fair, that's not the only way the plan went sideways."

"What else went wrong?" Kamenev asked.

"Kimiko was pretty convincing with the helmet and crossbow, but Marie somehow figured it out."

"Probably the way she walked or smelled," Irina guessed.

"Yeah, well whatever it was, it ate up some of the time I was hoping to give the other half of the team. I just about had a heart attack when she asked us to take off the helmets."

"You should not have worried," Irina said. "I found the tunnel immediately. The smell was obvious."

I looked at the little Russian beauty. "Then ...

why did it take you longer to get down there? What slowed you down?"

"She let some tourists take some pictures of her," Shaw guffawed. "I'm not kidding!"

My eyes looked into hers. "Why would you do that, Irina?"

"They liked the way I was dressed, and they asked." She brought a finger to her chin. "Perhaps it was the swords that made me look like I was in costume. It was only a couple of minutes."

Everyone laughed, and I winked at my Russian paramour. "Okay, so after the photos were done, the team found the tunnel and snuck up on Borges while his attention was on me."

"Very good," Kamenev said.

"Now, at this point, everything came together." I pointed to the Green Beret. "Shaw's M72 brought down some of the ceiling, and this gave us the separation we needed. Then, it was just a matter of destroying the old vampires and showing the newer vampires that there was a way out for them. And that's it. That was the whole plan."

My explanation was interrupted by two dark-haired women who walked into our assemblage. One I recognized right away. "Rosa!" I said loudly, and she smiled ear to ear. I looked at the woman beside her, and the resemblance was obvious to anyone. "Maria,

Is that you?"

The two women teared up and embraced me at the same time. "Thank you. Thank you all," Rosa said to the entire team. Everyone got up and went to the two sisters and embraced them. The two women seemed upset about Sergei's eye. They knew he lost it helping them. Maria seemed particularly interested in the handsome, bearded Russian. That brought a smile to my face.

Two gentlemen in suits walked up to us. The manager of the Beekman, Martin Scott, and Agent Boland. "Celebrating a job well done, I see," Scott said to the team with that twisted little smile. His eyes fell on the two sisters, and the smile ran away from his face. Maria took two quick steps and slapped him hard to make sure it wouldn't return. "You pig. *You knew!*" she shouted into his face.

Sergei moved between her and the manager, talking softly to her. The assistant manager, Steven Brown, came onto the scene.

"Good," I said, looking at Agent Boland. "We have one more thing to finish."

CHAPTER 41

The manager brought a hand to his reddening cheek and looked at Agent Boland. "Did you see that? She assaulted me!"

"I don't blame her," Boland replied with a smile on his face.

"What?" Scott spluttered.

I walked to stand in front of him. "Yeah, this is the final part of the job. Making sure this doesn't ever happen again."

The manager scowled at me. "What are you talking about?"

Agent Boland gestured to two large men, also in suits, at the other end of the bar. They didn't have any drinks, and they were on the job.

"What is this?" the manager growled.

Boland stepped forward and gave him the answer. "Mister Martin Scott, you are under arrest for drug possession, human trafficking, conspiracy to commit murder, the reckless endangerment of your employees, and probably a few other charges we haven't discovered yet."

"This is preposterous!" the manager protested.

"Look," I said to the man. "Borges was picking off staff in the hotel for years and probably would be doing it still, but your partner in crime stepped up his game, and that was the end of you."

"It's true," the assistant manager said. "We've gone through the records and the absences and number of employees who have gone missing ... it's inexplicable." Steven Brown looked down and frowned. "It's not how we take care of our people."

"Actually, it's not." Boland corrected him. "We went through the financials and found out Martin Scott was getting money on a monthly basis to look the other way while your hotel was used as a throughway for Borges, his wife, and his inner circle."

"You have no proof," Scott said, voice breaking.

Boland nodded his head. "Yeah, the money came from an account that belonged to a mister Claude Borges. The bank was quite shocked to see the account was almost two hundred years old."

"We told you!" Maria screamed over Sergei's shoulder. "We told you there was death in your hotel. We were afraid, and you sent us anyway!"

"I was just doing my job," the defeated manager muttered, looking at the floor.

"Really?" Boland laughed. "A hotel manager has no business owning that much cocaine. We found it in your home and in your desk." The lawman looked over at Irina. "Just like you said we would."

The Russian girl smiled and waved. "Happy to be helping!" she called.

"Get him out of here," Boland said to the big men, pulling Scott's arms behind his back. They cuffed him and walked him out of the bar. It was humiliating, and considering the evidence they had, it was final.

I looked at Boland. "What are you going to do with that nasty old vampire's bank account? I mean ... he's dead now."

"I can't say for sure. There's talk about distributing it amongst the survivors you guys saved. It's not my decision, but I like it."

"Me too," I said. "Look, we're going to be having a great time here tonight. Why not come back and have a few laughs with us?"

Boland pointed a finger at me. "Thanks for the offer, but I've got a wife and kid waiting for me at home."

"Good for you. Maybe next time," I said.

He offered me his hand. "Next time you're in New York, give me a call. I'd love to sit down and talk about what happened here today and anything else you want to share."

I shook his hand and grinned at him. "You got it. Have a great night, Agent Boland."

"You too, Medusa's Son," he said with a wink.

We both laughed, and I watched him go. I was surprised to see the assistant manager walk up to me and timidly offer a hand. Kamenev came to us, and he shook his hand, too. "Gentlemen," he said, clearing his throat. "The owner of the hotel extends his gratitude for a job well done, and he has invited you to stay in the hotel, free of charge, for two more days."

I looked at Kamenev and back at the small man. "Thank you, Mister Brown. Or should I say, Mister Steven Brown, manager of the Beekman Hotel?"

He grinned. "That is my new title." He looked around at our team and went back to Kamenev. "Enjoy your night and tip your servers well because the hotel is picking up the bill." He turned and walked away with a spring in his step.

"That ... is surprising considering what we were paid for this job," Kamenev said to me.

I shook my head. "I don't think that was the owner of the hotel who picked up this tab. I think it was the new manager." I looked at Kamenev. "Can you imagine working for a jerk like Martin Scott?"

Kamenev frowned. "Best not to think about such a thing. Better to celebrate what we have accomplished."

CHAPTER 42

The party went on and on, and everyone was having a time. Maria was totally enamored with Sergei. Maybe it was the eyepatch? It did make him look more interesting. To help things along, I walked to the two of them and looked at the young woman. "Are you going to give this guy your phone number? I mean … he's been winking at you all night." She was horrified, but Sergei's belly laugh helped her accept my bizarre sense of humor.

Shaw and Harada were sitting together, and I think I heard a little Japanese out of our Green Beret. It looked like Harada was teaching him or at least adding to his vocabulary. Amazing how people can find something in common when they have nothing in common. I think what I liked best was seeing Harada's face smile, and I even heard him laugh. He would still steal a glimpse at Kimiko, ever watchful for trouble, but he was having fun.

He wasn't the only one. Doctor Kimiko, Irina,

and Kim were tipping back fancy drinks and laughing with abandon. I had to smile. It wasn't that long ago that I had to defend the couple's relationship. Not an easy task for a traditional Russian woman whose moral compass was thirty-eight-years-old. But there she was ... not only giving them a chance but genuinely enjoying their company and sharing a laugh. I was proud of her and extremely impressed. I made a mental note to tell her that later.

Kamenev came and sat beside me, unbuttoning his immaculate suit jacket and exhaling as he sat. "Let's talk, Walt."

I pointed at the three ladies as they erupted in another laughing bout. "What do you suppose they're talking about?"

He shrugged and gave me a sly look. "Probably you."

We both laughed, and he put a big hand on my knee. "Are you happy with your decision?"

"Which one, Comrade?"

"You have made many decisions, Walt. Not that long ago, you decided to take my offer to help rid the world of this evil. Were you right? Did you make the right decision?"

It was a big question, and I had to admit that I hadn't really thought about it. But that was how my mind worked. When I make a decision, I don't make much of an effort to reflect on it. Now, I had a few drinks in me, and I had to consider the choice that I made. "You know ... I think it was the right decision, but I have a question for you, too."

"Please," he said, gesturing with his hand to ask what I wanted.

"How many did we save? How many people did Kimiko treat and have returned to their old lives? Because that's how I'm going to measure the success of that decision."

Kamenev looked at me and nodded very slowly. "The result of the decision. That is a good measure." He took a drink and looked at me. "Most of the vampires Kimiko inoculated survived."

"How many," I pressed.

"Two hundred and ten people are now living their lives. That many people owe their lives to you and the Medusa Division."

I let out a sigh and looked at the table. "Math has never been my strong suit, but that means we killed around ninety vampires. Is that right?"

The Russian smoothed out his tie and nodded. "That sounds about right, although there is no way to know for sure."

"I have to tell you, Mister Kamenev, I was hoping for better. Much better."

He laughed and shook his head. "I like you,

Walt. I do. But sometimes you are naïve to the ways of the world."

"What do you mean?"

He pointed a beefy finger at me and narrowed his eyes. "If you didn't answer the call and take this job, how many people would have been killed by the Borges?"

I took a drink and looked at him. "There is no possible way to know that."

Kamenev smiled, "Yes, that is true. But more were sure to die. Here is something else to consider. If local authorities found that lair, it would have been a war."

"That is true," I agreed quietly.

He put a hand on my knee again. "Walt, the SWAT teams here have the ammunition with your DNA. If you didn't act, they would have used it."

"Everyone would have died," I said with wide eyes.

"Yes, Walt. They would have killed every vampire in that chamber, including the two-hundred and ten souls now living their lives ... because of your decisions."

I held up my glass and smiled at him. The big Russian lifted his, and we clinked glasses. "To the Medusa Division," he said.

"The Medusa Division," I echoed as we both

took a drink. I looked at this man that I admired and respected and now I had a new feeling. Gratitude. "Thanks, Mister Kamenev. I really needed to hear that."

He leaned forward. "You are very welcome. But please ... call me Ivan," he growled with a smile.

I leaned forward and smiled, too. "*Nyet,*" I deadpanned.

He erupted in laughter and waved a hand at me as I leaned back, too. I started laughing, and the two of us enjoyed the lightest moment we'd had all week.

When we were done laughing, I leaned in and stole a quick glance to make sure nobody was listening to our conversation. "Actually, Mister Kamenev, there's another decision I've made, and I really need to run it by you."

CHAPTER 43

After sleeping like the dead, we woke and ordered room service for breakfast. We'd need the calories because we were taking on the city. Planning was probably the most fun part of the exercise. After a lot of discussion, we decided to see the Empire State Building but not go in it. Neither of us was particularly fond of heights, but it would be great to see and get a few pictures.

Times Square would be next. I asked Irina if she wanted to wear her battle gear and pose for pictures again. She threw a pillow at me. I took that as a "no." We would be the ones taking the pictures, and I was looking forward to that. Sure, I'd seen the place in a hundred pictures and movies, but to be there, to see it for yourself ...wow! I also wanted to see Irina's face when she saw it. Moscow was beautiful, but New York was ... well ... New York.

I think what excited us the most was seeing the famed Central Park. I just wanted to be able to say I was there, but Irina perked right up when we saw that it had a zoo. I forgot she was an animal lover. Vampires, she hated and killed. Animals she cherished and loved. That was my Irina, an enigma wrapped in a mystery.

After getting our fill of the amazing green space in the heart of the big city, we would check out the Metropolitan Museum of Art and the Guggenheim. As an artist, I was the worst. Even my stick men would get a failing grade. But I loved seeing it, being close enough to touch it. I wondered how it would affect Irina. Would her enhanced senses let her see the brush strokes? Maybe smell the canvas and paint? I was intrigued to see the effect of fine art on this miracle that had marched into my life and made a place in my heart.

There were certainly parks in Moscow. They had big rolling areas of green space. But again, Central Park was different. So many things to see and do, and she'd been in a walking nightmare for decades. If there was one person who deserved to see some fun and some beauty, it was Irina Kamenev.

After polishing off a fantastic breakfast, we bundled up and made our way down the elevator, through the bright atrium, and out the doors onto the street. We waved at the doorman, who greeted us, and I pulled out my phone to help us navigate.

Irina grabbed my arm, and I felt her mitten high on my bicep as we walked. "What are the others doing today?" she asked.

"Oh, Shaw was taking some of them on a tour of the city. Sergei, Harada, Maria, and Rosa are spending the day together."

She wrinkled her nose. "Harada surprises me. Isn't he watching over Kimiko?"

I laughed. "I think Kimiko wanted quality time with Kim. Couldn't have been easy to convince Harada to back up, but when she makes up her mind ... that's it."

"I like them," Irina announced. "We had such fun talking last night."

"That reminds me," I said, stopping and pulling her aside so the locals could walk by us. "I'm really proud of you for giving them a chance, Irina."

She tilted her head, and her bottom lip came out just a little. "What do you mean? I do not understand."

I smiled at her. "I know that when you were growing up in Russia over thirty years ago, there was no such thing as gay rights. I'm not so sure there are even now. But you looked past that and actually got to know them as people. You listened to me and gave them a chance."

"So what?" she asked, frowning at me.

"Well, that couldn't have been easy for you."

"Yes, it was."

I barked out a laugh and looked down into her

big, expressive eyes. "Really? A lot of people are not able to do that, you know. Letting go of past prejudices can be difficult."

She shrugged and tugged my arm to start us walking again. "It has been twenty years since I was a person. Things change. I realize this. Don't be stupid, Walt."

"Right," I said, biting my lip to stop myself from laughing. "I'm glad you see it's not a big deal."

She nodded her head as we walked. "It is not a big deal. It is simple. They love each other." Irina gave my arm a squeeze. "I love you, and you love me."

"True, true," I agreed. "It doesn't affect our lives in any way. It has nothing to do with us."

I saw her narrow her eyes and tilt her head as she looked up at me. "Yes, if Kimiko loved you, then I would have to kill her."

My feet stopped moving, and I stared down at her with my mouth open. She was smiling at me. "I make joke. I am kidding, Walt."

I let out a sigh and started walking again. I could see the Empire State Building coming up. "Thank God," I mumbled.

She stopped me and turned me to face her. She gave me a quick peck on the lips. "I make joke, but you are mine."

"Great," I laughed, pointing at the big building.

"And that is our first stop."

****

The Empire State Building did not disappoint. The majestic building, built in 1931, was a majestic, monstrous Art Deco masterpiece. Looking up at it was dizzying, and we both grinned as we stood as close as we could and looked up. I'm sure people walking by thought we were foolish tourists, but we didn't care. Why should we?

Times Square was bright, busy, and just standing there was a thrill. The huge, flashing electronic billboards, the crowds of people, and what delighted us most were the costumed characters milling around. I was glad I brought cash because Irina wanted a picture with all of them. It was going to be hilarious to look at the pictures later. The smile never left her face, and she laughed and laughed between every picture.

I felt like I wasn't even a part of this moment. It was like I wasn't there; I was just watching it. And Irina … was amazed and amazing. Maybe losing twenty years of your life gave someone a new appreciation for the little things. She giggled and complimented every street performer. She danced for every busker and took the time to watch every commercial on every screen, no matter what it was for. She was adorable, and I caught more than a few people trying not to smile as they watched her joy. Even the police on horseback were touched when she took a moment to talk to them … and their horses. It was all I could do to get her to leave, but I'm glad I did.

Her sensitive ears picked up on it long before I was able to detect it. "That music …" she whispered and ran ahead of me into Central Park. It took me a few minutes before I heard it too, and I ran to catch up with her. I wasn't missing this.

The simulated pipe organ pushing joy greeted my ears, and I also heard the laughter and screaming of children. I scanned the crowd, not because I was worried about her, but because I wanted to see what she was doing. It was sure to be memorable.

I found her looking at the carousel, hands on the fence, and just jumping up and down with excitement. She looked at me, and there were tears in her eyes. "Can we?" She called to me as I walked up to the old ride.

Five minutes later, we had done our time in line, and we were on a wooden horse, going up and down. The energetic carousel music matched the smile on her face perfectly. She grinned and looked around as we went up and down, around and around. When the ride finally came to a stop, she looked at me, and her eyes were huge. She grabbed my arm and shouted, "Again!"

Six rides on the carousel later, we were on our

way to the Gapstow Bridge.

CHAPTER 44

I'd heard about this bridge, but I'd never seen it. It was ancient, made of big, chunky, grey rocks, and there was a tree beside it that had lost all its leaves. Its branches were like black fingers reaching into the hazy winter sky. The bridge was reflected in the smooth, still water it spanned.

Irina and I came to the center of the bridge and looked out over the water. "It is beautiful," she whispered.

"It really is," I said. I looked at her. "Thanks, Irina. I really needed this. These last few weeks have been difficult. Training, the mission. All of it."

She snuggled closer. "It has been hard for you."

"It has." I put an arm around her. "I can make decisions. I've never been indecisive. But ... I've never had to make such important choices. People's lives depended on what I decided. That is huge."

"You did well, Walt. It was good outcome, yes?" she said.

"I think so. I still run different scenarios through my head. I wonder if I could have gotten Claude Borges to surrender. Maybe I should have walked right into that big chamber and given all of the older vampires a chance."

She shook her head. "Nyet, they would not have defied their master. Until that monster was dead, they had no chance. You did right."

"I know," I whispered. "I always get back to that same conclusion. There was no other way."

"I am glad," she answered. "Living with regret, it is not living. It is carrying a burden that you cannot put down."

I looked at her and smiled. "I feel the same way. The hard decisions must be made, and it won't ever get easier. Leading the Medusa Division will mean more of that. But some decisions are easier than others. Some decisions are not really decisions at all. Sometimes, you're just doing what you know you must be done. Some things are inevitable, but no less surprising and wonderful."

She frowned at me. "I do not understand these words."

"Let me help," I said, looking into those dark, liquid eyes. I reached into my pocket and found the small velvet box I'd been carrying for days. I took a knee as I pulled it out and took her hand in mine while the other hand held the small container.

Her eyes were wide as I looked up at her. "Walt, what are you doing?" she asked.

"I'm doing the best thing I've ever done. I'm making the easiest decision that I've ever had to make. It's one that I feel the universe has made for me, and I'm glad." I opened the box so she could see the ring. "Irina Kamenev ... will you marry me?"

Her face fell, and her eyes bulged. "Are you serious? Is this joke?"

There I was, on one knee, looking up at everything I ever wanted. My knee was starting to ache, and I felt a little weird kneeling on the bridge as people walked by. I looked left, then right, and back at the beautiful young woman in front of me. "Irina ... this is the part where you give me an answer."

A hefty jogger in an old grey tracksuit with wild, curly hair ran by us on the old bridge. "Say yes!" he shouted over his shoulder as he went by, giving us a thumbs-up.

We both started laughing at the absurdity of the situation. "Well, are you going to listen to the random fat guy that just ran by?" I asked her. "Can I have an answer?"

"Yes! Yes, I will marry you!" she cried, and I stood up. We kissed, and I helped her put on the ring. It was a little too large to fit on her ring finger, so we put it back in the box and in my pocket. "When did you get this ring?" she asked.

"When we were at the jewelers, getting your necklace and earrings. Remember when you went to the washroom?"

She gave me a playful swat. "That was sneaky."

"Yes, it was."

"I cannot wait to tell Papa," she said, and gave me a big hug.

"Oh, well … he already knows."

She let go of me and stepped back. "How can he know about this? You told him?"

"Irina, it is traditional for a young man to get permission from a young lady's father to ask for her hand in marriage."

She frowned. "But it is my decision. That is stupid tradition."

"Uh, maybe. But it's still tradition. I'd have asked even if he didn't give his blessing, but he was all for it."

It was fun watching her wrestle with this. "I cannot believe he knew … I will still be glad to see him, and he will want to celebrate."

"You're right," I laughed. "He's at the Russian Consulate on 5th Street and East 91st. He wants to take us out to celebrate. How does that sound?"

"It sounds wonderful!" she cheered, throwing

her arms around me and picking me up. She easily twirled us around, carrying me like a big stuffed bear. A couple walking by stared at the small woman's feat of strength, and she put me down, still laughing.

"Let's go," I said, offering her my arm. She took it, and we started walking.

I was thinking that I would never, ever call her father "Ivan." I would have to call him "Papa." Now, *that* was going to be fun.

"I almost forgot," I said as we moved closer to the Russian Consulate. "Your father wants to talk to us about our next assignment."

"So soon? We just finished mission," she complained.

"Yeah, I know what you mean. This one sounds wild."

"Where is this mission? Where are we going?"

I let out a sigh. "Where it all began, Croatia."

"Where you were born?" She asked.

"Where vampires started, and yes … where I was born."

We walked a little further. Irina must have heard the tension in my voice. She stopped me and gave me another good, tight hug. "It will be alright, Walt."

"Will it? Because it feels like 'Medusa's Son,' going to the place that spawned the infection that makes vampires is going to get messy."

She took my face in her hands and looked up into my eyes. "It will be alright because you will have your team. You will have your wits, and you will have me." She kissed me on the lips lightly. "Okay?"

I smiled down at my little angel of death. "Oh, I'm not worried for us. I'm worried about anyone that gets in your way."

She laughed. "Come on, Papa is waiting. He will be so happy."

And this was the miracle of it all. Not the amazing things she could do or the fact that something in me destroys vampires. Not even that we had saved so many lives on this crazy mission.

No. The miracle of it all was that this wonderful woman chose me. We found each other in a sterile lab where she was to be destroyed in the interests of science. From the moment I put my hand on the glass of her cell and she raised her hand to meet it, we were headed to this destination. This amazing, beautiful woman decided that I was the one for her. She fell in love with me, and she allowed me to fall for her.

She was no longer my girlfriend; she was my fiancée. I was no longer thinking about the Medusa Division. I was thinking of our union. I didn't know what the future held, but I knew I wouldn't have to face it alone. That much was certain.

Author Ian Mitchell-Gill has lived a rich and varied life that made writing almost inevitable. Born overseas and raised in rural Canada, his days were spent playing guitar, engaging in athletic endeavors, and reading every paperback jammed on the shelves. Surrounded by great storytellers in his family and a close-knit group of friends, allowed his imagination to roam.

This path led him down the road to becoming a teacher, and he started writing to create samples for his students to understand how a story is developed and polished. He and his students enjoyed the process so much that he began to write a chapter a week to share with them.

His many experiences and interests proved to be valuable background for some of the characters and situations in the book.

Ian lives in Oshawa, Ontario, with his wife and two daughters. He continues to teach.